"Charming, wit[h] chance romance [and] snappy banter lef[t] ...race from the start. Karmen Lee has created the perfect formula—fiery tension, palpable chemistry and the willingness to forgive—leaving readers with what we love most: The ultimate HEA."

—Author Denise N. Wheatley on *The 7-10 Split*

"Loaded with wit, unrealized feelings, and unresolved history, Lee's *7-10 Split* delights and elevates a bowling rivalry between the cutest pairing with a striking side of steam."

—Kelly Cain, author of *An Acquired Taste*, on *The 7-10 Split*

"Brimming with heart and humor, this second chance romance has it all—rivalry, tension, chemistry, longing, and of course, more than a few tricky 7-10 splits. A breathtaking, heartwarming romance."

—Ashley Herring Blake, award-winning author of *Delilah Green Doesn't Care*, on *The 7-10 Split*

"Lee's (*Passion Over Pride*) slow-burn second-chance romance makes a great addition to the Afterglow line and is sure to leave readers anxiously anticipating the next book in the series."

—*Library Journal* on *The 7-10 Split*

"Lee does a great job balancing the characters' past and present. Their history is always lingering in the background, and when it comes to the foreground, it's that much more powerful, because it never feels like it's coming out of nowhere."

—*Autostraddle* on *The 7-10 Split*

"[Such] HAWT sex scenes.... Every touch, kiss, caress, feels incredibly real and deliciously sexy. There is something extra sensual about the way Black women love on each other sexually, and I think [the author] captured that sensuality so perfectly. I was absolutely fanning myself after each sex scene."

—*Autostraddle* on *The 7-10 Split*

Also by Karmen Lee

The 7-10 Split
The Relationship Mechanic

Visit the Author Profile page at Harlequin.com for more titles.

The Secret Crush Book Club

KARMEN LEE

ISBN-13: 978-1-335-50722-8

The Secret Crush Book Club

Harlequin Enterprises ULC
22 Adelaide St. West, 41st Floor
Toronto, Ontario M5H 4E3, Canada
www.Harlequin.com

HarperCollins Publishers
Macken House, 39/40 Mayor Street Upper,
Dublin 1, D01 C9W8, Ireland
www.HarperCollins.com

Printed in U.S.A.

Recycling programs for this product may not exist in your area.

One

The house was quiet. Too quiet. The once-familiar sounds of her sisters arguing, and their father, Daniel, caught in the cross fire of trying to calm them down, was now replaced with uncomfortable silence. Once upon a time, Dani had prayed for peace so she could at least hear herself think, but now the only sound seemed to come from her own breathing. She was quickly finding that she hated it.

Finishing a day of work should have been a good thing, and overall, it was. But with Jordan at the library, and the rest of the family scattered about, Dani was bored. It was a Thursday evening and if not working the evening shift, most of her friends were home with their families. Now that she worked the day shift, she had evenings free and fuck all to fill them with.

"Well, this was not what I was expecting," Dani muttered to herself as she changed the television channel again. There was nothing to watch. Nothing to do. Sleeping this early would mean waking up far before dawn, and that still left the next two days for her to get through. Having Friday and Saturday off was coveted, so she was trying hard not to be ungrateful. She worked with several other nurses who would gladly take the time from her if she asked. They would also, no doubt, have more ideas on what to do with the time off than she did, which was a whole lot of nothing.

"Hey, kiddo. What are you doing staring off into space?"

Dani smiled and looked up. "Just contemplating homicide. Trying to decide if I should bury the body or take some time off to drive down and drop it in the Everglades."

With a snort, Daniel walked over to her. "Maybe you should let whoever live. You're too cute to go to prison." He dropped a brief kiss on her forehead.

"Only going to prison if I get caught," Dani replied. She took a moment to get a good look at him. "Where are you going in your Sunday best?"

He shook his head, but his lips quirked up in a smile. "It's seniors' night down at the rec center, and I told Clarence and Prichard I'd meet them there."

That was news to her. Still, as unexpected as that tidbit was, she was glad he was getting out and not spending all his time alone in the house. Kind of like Dani was doing now. *Damn. Even Dad has more of a social life than me.* The thought was disconcerting.

"Well, you have fun and don't do anything I wouldn't do."

He raised an eyebrow at her, but eventually left. Dani heard his ancient Ford truck start up and once the sound faded away, she realized she was once again sitting alone with only the television for company. This was starting to become a pattern. With a sigh, Dani pushed up off the couch and grabbed her keys. There was no point in sitting around the house.

She stewed in her thoughts the whole drive to the library. Jordan spent several nights a week there. He had joined their esports club last year and enjoyed it so much he kept it up. Dani hadn't known what to think of the whole thing. When she was his age, video games were something they did alone or with just a few friends at someone's house. There weren't actual clubs dedicated to it. When her dad had heard about it, he had joked about how the world had changed. When she realized how similar they had sounded, she had almost gagged at realizing that she had become her parents. It was a terrifying revelation, but one she refused to dwell on. She was still young. She was still hip.

Do kids these days even say hip *anymore?* She had no idea.

She pulled off the road at the gas station to fill up the car and grab a snack for herself and Jordan. The kid was going through another growth spurt, which meant not only was she going to have to once again replace his entire wardrobe, but also if he didn't have something to nibble on every hour or so, he turned into an absolute beast.

Inside the gas station, she went straight to the chips and grabbed a couple of their favorites, and chose a couple of sodas to wash them down after. When she got in line, she jolted as her name was called by a familiar voice.

"Dani?"

Fixing a fake-feeling smile on her face, she turned slowly and came face-to-face with Zavier. She had gone out with him a few times last month before realizing that the chemistry she had been hoping for was just not there. He was a nice enough guy, but boring. If not for the fact that he had impeccable taste in choosing restaurants, she probably wouldn't have gone out with him a second and then a third time. She had paid for her own meals each time, so she didn't feel as guilty as she would have if he'd covered everything, but she still felt bad when she admitted that she didn't see things going any further. He had taken it well, thankfully.

"Oh, Zavier. I didn't see you come in." She winced internally at how awkward that sounded. When the cashier called her to come forward, Dani latched on to that. She hoped he didn't say anything more, but that hope was dashed as he spoke up again.

"How are you doing?"

She half turned, trying to convey she was busy without seeming rude. "I'm doing great." There was a moment where neither of them spoke before she begrudgingly spoke up again. "How are you doing?"

"Great," he replied with a wide smile. Dani hoped that he didn't think she was giving him another way in. "I got the promotion I was telling you about. I'm Miami-bound in a couple weeks."

"That's awesome." She truly did think that was great for him, but it just highlighted another reason why she knew things wouldn't have worked out. The farthest she had lived for any amount of time was Atlanta for a year and a half for college before circumstances had her returning home. Regardless, it had only taken a few months for her to realize that big-city living was not something she wanted. Peach Blossom was home for Dani. Sure, she liked vacations as much as the next person, but she had no desire to be anywhere else. "I've heard Miami is a great city." She grabbed her purchases. "Sorry, I have to head out to pick up Jordan. It was great seeing you."

He called out his own goodbyes as she made her way outside, and Dani was relieved to see he was parked on the other side away from her. She concentrated on getting her gas before hopping back in the car and driving off.

When she pulled into the library parking lot, the sun was slowly dipping beyond the horizon, but it was still pleasantly warm outside. Spring was slowly melting into summer, and soon enough she knew it would be hot and too humid to stand. She was already regretting wearing jeans instead of grabbing a pair of shorts when she had changed out of her scrubs. Spending so much time in uniform meant she rarely knew what to wear outside of it. Usually she got home, showered and changed into pajamas for the rest of the night. But now that Vini was out of the country with Jessica on some whirlwind vacation, and Ava and Grace were joined at the ass more often than not, she was the one picking Jordan up from the library in the evenings. It wasn't a bad thing, considering he was her kid after all, but it was just another reminder that things were slowly but surely changing in the Williams household.

Inside, the library was cool, and Dani fluttered her eyes as she let the refreshing air rush over her. It was quiet in the way most libraries were, and she paused just inside the door, not quite sure where she should go. It wasn't like she never came in. She had picked Jordan up earlier in the week, so she knew where he was. But she was early, and she knew he would not appreciate being interrupted or having to stop early. The kid was serious when it came to his gaming, and since she was paying for him to participate, she had no desire to cut his time short. With a sigh, she headed to the counter.

"Hey, Zoey."

The library's newest librarian blinked quickly before her lips turned up in a soft smile. She had been the one to start the esports program when she had moved to Peach Blossom a little over five months ago, and if you asked Jordan, the sun shone out of her ass. After the first meeting, he had come home so energized that Dani almost didn't know what to do with him. He had spoken of nothing but Zoey for that first month and even now, almost half a year later, he still had nothing but good things to say about her.

"Hi, Dani," she replied, her voice pitched soft enough that Dani almost had to lean forward to catch it. For someone as tall as she was, Dani had been surprised that

Zoey was so soft-spoken when she'd first met her. "You're here early."

That was certainly true. Dani had only a vague idea of her plans when she had made her way to the library, but now that she was here, she couldn't exactly recall what she wanted to do.

"Did you need help with something?"

Did she ever. "Probably need help with my entire life." She hadn't meant to say that out loud, but it was out there now. Zoey's eyes widened behind her black square-shaped frames, but Dani figured she might as well keep on going. "Got any books to help someone through a quarter-life crisis? They aren't my usual go-to when I grab a book. I'd much rather read another banger from Caitlyn Martin and lose myself in someone else's drama instead of my own, but it is what it is."

"Um," Zoey stammered as she looked down at the computer in front of her. She typed in a few things before pausing and looking up at Dani from over the rims of her glasses. "We have some self-help books if that's what you're looking for?"

Figuring that she had traumatized the poor woman enough, Dani nodded. Self-help is probably what she needed anyway. Maybe she could find a book to help explain why she felt so upended lately.

"That would be great. Could you point me in the direction of that section?"

"Sure," Zoey replied, nodding. "Or... I could show

you to it? I have some books I need to put away in that area anyway."

"If you don't mind."

She shook her head, smiling again. "I'd love to. It's what I'm here for after all." Zoey signaled to the other librarian before walking around the counter and toward Dani. She gestured for her to follow.

Peach Blossom's library wasn't the largest, but it did have two levels. Dani hadn't spent much time there even with Jordan coming multiple times a week. She usually just waited for him outside or went straight to the conference room they always occupied. As much as Dani loved to read, she usually got her books delivered to her e-reader or purchased them online. Going to the library or waiting for a book to be available always seemed like a waste of time before. When they turned down another aisle, Dani caught another glimpse of Zoey in her glasses.

"Those look really cute on you."

"What?"

"Your glasses," Dani elaborated. When Zoey stopped walking and faced her more fully, she knew exactly who the glasses reminded her of. "You look like a sexy Black version of Velma. Especially with the cardigan."

Zoey's eyes widened. "Oh! Um, thank you." She looked down and for a moment, Dani worried that she had offended her. Before she could say anything, Zoey gestured at the books on the shelf. "These are all the self-help. I wasn't sure which ones you really wanted to browse, but there are a lot of great titles to choose from."

Dani smiled, gently hoping that she looked harmless enough. She hadn't meant to embarrass the other woman. Clearly, she needed to work on her socializing skills if she was going to go out in public more. "I'm sure I can find something, though it would be easier if there was a title specifically about quarter-life crises." When Zoey didn't say anything, Dani internally sighed and vowed to look up a book on how to not make things fucking awkward. "Thanks, Zoey. I appreciate you helping me."

Zoey nodded before taking a step backward. When Dani turned to look at the books in front of her, Zoey's voice caught her attention.

"It'll be okay."

Dani furrowed her brow, not sure how to respond. Her silence must have worried Zoey into speaking up again.

"Everyone has moments like that," Zoey continued. "Where they aren't sure about the way their life is going. But it's okay, I think. No one said you have to have everything figured out."

It was the longest conversation the two of them had ever really had, and Dani felt something shift. The words weren't overwhelmingly positive or poetic, but they were said firmly enough to catch Dani's thoughts and leave her speechless on how to respond. By the time she finally formed words, Zoey had already turned and walked away, leaving Dani standing alone, gaze locked on her retreating frame.

Two

Oh my god. That was all Zoey could think as she made a strategic retreat from where she had left Dani in the aisle. They had finally had an entire conversation, and here she was running away after letting her mouth get away from her. What the hell had she been thinking, imparting that last little bit of wisdom like she was some great sage. Just because she was an author, didn't mean she knew the right words to say—especially in the face of the one woman who had caught her eye months ago. This pining thing was for the birds.

"I didn't expect you to be back so soon," Tiffany said. She had a knowing look on her face and a smirk on her lips, but Zoey didn't even feel like rising to the bait. She was still too stuck on the fact that she had had a chance, a real chance to say something to Dani, and yet she choked. She choked hard. As if hearing her thoughts, Tiffany cocked her head and looked more deeply at Dani. "Why do you look so shell-shocked? What happened?"

Zoey walked around the counter and dropped down into the chair they kept back there for when someone got tired of standing. "It was awful."

"What? Why? Did she tell you books were stupid?"

"Of course not," Zoey countered. She covered her face with her hands briefly as she gathered herself. "So, you know how she asked me for help finding some books?"

Tiffany nodded. "Something about self-help. I'm not a fan of those myself, but it is what it is. Did she change her mind or something? Did she decide she needed to go all 'finding herself in a tropical place and changing religions' on you?"

"I don't know where you even come up with these things. No, she was happy to look through the books I showed her, but then she was talking, and she seemed so down so I..." Zoey could feel her stomach clench in embarrassment as she thought about her words. If not for already having a book deal, she would have given up her dream of being an author right then.

"You what?" Tiffany prompted. "Spit it out already. You're making me so nervous that I might have to call the cops or something."

Zoey groaned. "I told her that everything is going to be okay."

Tiffany stared at her for a moment before she frowned. "Are you serious right now? That's all? I thought you had done something crazy, like tell her she should sell all her things and move to Antarctica to commune with penguins or something." She rolled her eyes before reaching for the stack of books in front of her. "Your overdramatic ass should have been an actress instead of a librarian."

Zoey thought that was a little uncalled for until she realized that she had essentially just had a breakdown about having a single conversation. This was not a great way to start things. "I'm not trying to be dramatic." When Tiffany gave her a look, she insisted, "I'm not. It's just…" She didn't exactly know how to describe how she was feeling. It wasn't often that she liked someone to the point of wanting to do something about it. Not since her sort-of-but-not-quite ex-girlfriend had she felt the need to pursue someone. The vagueness of that relationship and the abrupt way it had blown apart left her hesitant to even try dating in the year since. As a result, she now found herself ill-equipped when it came to expressing interest without feeling like a fish flapping about on the shore.

"How am I supposed to approach her?"

"Walk up to her and just tell her she smells pretty or something." Tiffany's flippant response had Zoey scowling. This wasn't the time to make fun of her. She had a real issue. "Seriously. There's no magic word for this. I know you've approached people before. You're a librarian. We talk to people all the time."

"We talk to patrons all the time. Or kids. Not attractive women who make our blood burn and our ears ring."

Tiffany grinned. "That was almost poetic." When Zoey took a swipe at her, she moved out of range with a smile. "You should write that down and send it to her. Bring back old school love letters and all that."

Zoey tried to ignore how much she liked that idea. It wouldn't be smart to show too much interest in one of Tiffany's harebrained schemes. That way only led to madness, and she wasn't trying to have her business splashed through the town gossip train. She shook her head to dispel that thought. This was not the time for idle daydreams. This was a time to be serious.

"I can't do that," she said. It was then a thought struck her. "Oh no!"

"What?" Tiffany asked looking around. "What happened?"

Zoey widened her eyes. "She told me she liked my books, and I didn't stop to tell her they were mine. What do I say if she brings them up again? What if she thinks I'm weird because I didn't come clean immediately? What if she thinks I'm bragging if I say I wrote them?"

Tiffany held up a hand, halting the flow of her words. "First of all, slow down. All the questions are giving me whiplash. Second, just come clean and tell her you are her author in shining foiled cover. I guarantee that she'll be excited if she likes them as much as you said she does."

The thought sounded good. It was a dream of Zoey's to be well-known and recognized for her writing. But to do that would also mean divulging a picture of herself at the very least. She had three books under her belt and was working on her fourth, but she had always been very deliberate about keeping her personal life and writing persona separate. She didn't have an actual author photo, and instead used artwork gifted to her from a fellow author. It wasn't that she never planned on coming out and showing who she was, but it had never seemed like the right time. Actually, that was a lie. She had wanted to be anonymous for her whole career, but now that she knew Dani was a fan, she was seriously considering giving up on that path.

Zoey sighed. She wasn't the best at social situations despite her public-facing job. Books were easy. People, not so much. Right when she struggled to find something to say, commotion from the back conference room caught her attention.

"What in the world is going on back there?" Tiffany asked with raised brows. When an older woman walked over to the desk, Zoey gestured to the noise.

"I'll check on the boys if you'll handle the desk?" She wasn't surprised when Tiffany agreed eagerly. The esports team was a joint effort in name only. Tiffany didn't know or care about gaming. She had thrown her name down only because she agreed that they needed to do what they could to keep kids coming into the library. The setup for the team had cost a pretty penny, but she and Zoey both agreed that the impact far outweighed the dent in their budget.

Zoey pushed the conversation with Dani out of her mind as she headed toward the back. Things were still quiet overall, but when another burst of noise erupted from the room, she put more pep in her step. She wasn't expecting chaos when she opened the door.

"What is going on in here?"

The boys were mostly standing with headsets still on as they loudly talked over one another. She couldn't understand everything that was being said, but she took a step inside and closed the door behind her to keep most of the argument in the room and not spilling out into the rest of the library.

Zoey knew all of the boys. She had been the one to approve them joining the club after all. In the middle of the fray was Jordan, Dani's son. Zoey was surprised to hear him raising his voice like the others. Usually, he was the calm, levelheaded one. He had been appointed a sort of captain by the rest of the boys, so she was more than a little concerned with how worked up he seemed to be getting.

"Boys," she said, raising her voice over theirs to be heard. It wasn't a tone she often felt the need to use, and it had nothing on what she and Tiffany referred to as the "mom voice" that patrons sometimes used when their kids were being a little too boisterous for the library, but it would have to do. The boys all seemed to hesitate when they realized she was standing there. Jordan, in particular, looked relieved. "Have you all forgotten you're in a library?" she continued.

"No, ma'am," they replied almost in unison. Their voices were contrite, though some of them were still cutting each other scathing looks. Keeping up her stern persona, Zoey crossed her arms over her chest and peered down at them from behind her lenses.

"Good. Now, tell me what in the world is going on in

here." She held a hand up when multiple mouths opened. "One of you at a time. I can't understand anything with you all talking at once."

They looked at one another before all turning to look at Jordan. He sighed before taking a step forward. "Griffin thinks Jason was using a cheat code. I wasn't sure, so I said we should just restart the round."

"I wasn't cheating!"

"There's no way you're that good!"

"Boys," Zoey exclaimed, stopping the argument before it started again. They both fell quiet, though they frowned and cut their eyes at one another. Thankfully, the others seemed content to let her handle it, rather than jump in with their thoughts. That was good. She didn't need all of them getting riled up again. "I agree that if there was a legitimate concern about cheating, then starting the round over again was the best way to go."

Jordan smiled and ducked his head. Zoey couldn't help but smile over at him.

"Cheating during a tournament, or even outside of it, is a good way to get yourself banned from the servers and then it won't matter how good you are," she said pitching her voice to include all of them and not just Griffin and Jason. It had the effect she was hoping for, and they all paid attention. "But, just because someone is doing better than you think they should, that doesn't mean they are cheating. You all are teammates. Don't forget that."

Her phone beeped and Zoey pulled it from her cardigan's pocket. It was time for more of the parents to start arriving. She clapped her hands, getting their attention again. "Alright. It's time to clean up and get ready for pickup." The boys grumbled, but they all moved, cleaning up the stations and pushing in their chairs. Right on time, the first knock came on the door before it opened, and a parent stuck their head into the room.

The boys steadily moved out of the room as they were picked up by their parents until only Jordan was left. When he started helping out by cleaning up around the computers and making sure everything was powered down, Zoey thanked him. He really was a good kid, and she understood exactly why the others often looked to him to settle things.

"Your mom should be here in just a bit," Zoey said after the last chair had been pushed in. "I was actually helping her find some books earlier and I doubt she would have left without you."

Jordan chuckled. "She probably got lost figuring out which aisle to turn down. Directions aren't her superpower."

Zoey giggled softly before shushing him. "Don't let your mom hear you say that."

"Too late." Dani's voice made Zoey freeze, and before she could thaw out, Jordan had already moved around her to the door. When she turned, Dani was looking at her with a tilted smile. "I'll have you know, I only got lost in a library once, and it was because I was reading and walking instead of paying attention."

"That's an easy mistake to make," Zoey said in agreement. She took a step closer to the door before pausing. "Our library is small enough that it probably won't be an issue though."

Dani shrugged, her smile still pasted on her face. "You'd be surprised what can happen when you're distracted." She looked down at Jordan before putting a hand on his shoulder. "How did this one do today? Hopefully he didn't give you any trouble."

Zoey shook her head. "He never does. Jordan is definitely a good one. And I really appreciated his help today when it came to solving a minor disagreement between the boys."

Jordan looked up at Dani with a smirk. "See. I told you I'm a joy to have around." When Dani rolled her eyes, Zoey couldn't contain her snort of laughter.

Dani's gaze fixed on her then, her smile looking soft and filled with a fondness that made Zoey's breath catch. It was almost unfair how gorgeous Dani was, with her rich brown skin and angular features. Her brown eyes were warm, and Zoey just wanted to sink into them and never look away.

"Can we stop at Thomas's on the way home? I'm hungry."

Jordan's voice reminded Zoey that she was not, in fact, in a world with just her and Dani. She wasn't sure how long they had stood there looking at one another, but just the thought of being caught gawking at her was enough to have Zoey's cheeks heating up. Dani blinked slowly before she nodded to Jordan.

"Sure," she replied. "I didn't feel like cooking anyway. It was good to see you again, Zoey." Jordan was tugging her away, no doubt eager to get dinner quickly. She knew how quickly kids grew. Even though she didn't have any herself, she had been around enough of them to know that once they hit middle school, their appetites ramped up and they essentially became vacuum cleaners for food.

"It was good to see you too," Zoey called out as Dani was pulled from the room. She answered Dani's little wave with one of her own, but as she watched them walk away, she knew she had to do something. Tiffany's words rang in her mind, but that was too much too soon for her. She had to think of something else, and quickly.

"Dani, wait!" Zoey winced at the volume of her voice. She had broken her own library rule about being too loud, but she couldn't let Dani go just yet. When she reached them, she quickly pulled a pen and a slip of paper from her pocket. "I'm not sure if you would even be interested, but if you like books, I have a book club each week at my house. We're starting a new book this month, so it's sort of the perfect time to join us."

Before her courage could fail her, Zoey jotted her cell on the paper and held it out to Dani. When Dani took it, their fingers brushed, and Zoey had to stop herself from melting right then at that warm touch. Dani looked down at the paper before looking back up at her.

"Thanks."

"Of course," Zoey said, trying not to sound as breathless as she felt. "No pressure."

Another pull from Jordan had Dani moving again, and Zoey tried her best not to stare as she left. If she spent the next couple days incessantly checking her phone and hoping it was Dani, that was no one's business but her own.

Three

"Time differences are going to be the death of me, I swear," Dani muttered as she waited for her sister Vini's face to appear on the screen. She had missed the timing yesterday, but she was determined to get it right today.

Vini and her girlfriend, Jessica, had only been in Korea to visit Jessica's family for a few days so far, but the pictures Vini had sent already had Dani wishing she had the time off to follow them over there. The only international destinations she had ever been to were drivable— granted, Toronto would have been a daunting trek. Still, she hadn't ever set foot off the continent, and she was itching to find the time to do so. When the call finally connected and Vini's face appeared on the screen, Dani couldn't help but feel relieved. She didn't doubt Jessica was taking excellent care of Vini, but it still soothed the big-sister part of Dani that Vini's wide smile meant she was having a great time. After years of practically being joined at the hip, she figured she could be forgiven for being a bit overprotective. She didn't show that side like their sister Ava did by being overprotective, sometimes to the point of overstepping boundaries, but it was there all the same.

"It's about time you answered," Dani said, covering her excitement with a smart-ass remark. It wouldn't do to seem soft right off the bat. That would only worry Vini, and as much as Dani missed her, she was happy she was finally getting out there and acting her age.

Vini's smile was radiant. "Oh, I'm sorry. Were you missing me?"

Dani rolled her eyes but didn't deny it. "Of course I missed you," she admitted. "Now who will I take my car to for an oil change?"

Vini's laughter made Dani's chest warm, and she switched the phone to her other hand as she relaxed back on the sofa. Vini shook her head, eyes crinkling at the sides with her grin. "You won't need an oil change for at least another three thousand miles. What are you planning on doing? Driving to Miami or something?"

"You never know."

"Don't make me have to call Jordan on you," Vini joked.

Dani rolled her eyes again. "I am a grown-ass woman who can do what she grown ass pleases."

Vini snorted. "Sure. Keep telling yourself that. How are things going there?"

"Things are totally fine. Nothing new to report," Dani

replied, almost sighing at how true that was. She enjoyed small-town living, and she couldn't see herself living anywhere but Peach Blossom really. But sometimes things were a little too quiet—a little too slow, leaving her feeling restless with the itch to go somewhere, anywhere just to see something unfamiliar. "Though, I'm kind of hoping you convince Jessica to move to Peach Blossom and open up a Korean restaurant. The food pictures you keep sending are making me hungry. I'm tempted to go up to Atlanta just for BBQ. I've never driven that far just for some damn meat before in my life."

Vini gagged, making Dani laugh. "That's not what I want to hear from you."

"So, you want to hear how far I did drive for meat?"

"No," Vini exclaimed. Dani heard giggling in the background, and she figured it was Jessica. "I don't want to hear anything about you and meat, or meat in general. When did you get so vulgar?"

"Birth," Dani replied simply. "I'm glad you're having a great time though. What are your plans for today?"

Vini's enthusiasm kept Dani's spirits high. She really was happy for her sister, but it just left her feeling a strange sense of jealousy, especially when Jessica finally popped in the frame and gave Vini a kiss on her forehead. The two of them looked so cozy that Dani almost felt guilty about her jealousy. She knew it was natural to sometimes feel this way, but damn if it didn't smart.

"How's Aiden doing?" Vini asked. "He hasn't burnt down my shop yet, has he?"

Dani knew she was joking. Aiden was more than competent enough to run things while Vini was away. If he wasn't, then she wouldn't even have considered going. That shop was Vini's baby.

"Was still standing when I drove by the other day. Next time, I'll tell Ava to go check."

Vini waved the suggestion away. "Nah, she's probably too busy with Grace. Just drive by again when you can. I'm sure it'll all be fine, but it feels weird to not be there, you know?" Dani wasn't sure how to respond to that. She didn't own her own business, so she didn't feel any anxiety about leaving the office.

Dani was a little annoyed though. Why would Vini think Ava was too busy, but Dani wasn't? Just because she didn't have a girlfriend to gallivant all over town with didn't mean she didn't have other things to do. Important things. Things that might take up her time. She did have a child after all.

Vini looked away for a moment before turning back to the phone. "I have to go, sis. We're packing to go catch our train down to Busan. Jessica's cousin lives there and is eager to meet me. He apparently collects vintage cars and wants to hang out."

Dani chuckled. "Figures you would go halfway around the world and still be talking shop. Watch out for any zombies. Give Jessica my love and keep sending me those food pictures."

Vini saluted with a smile. "You got it, sis."

"I'll take good care of her, D. Promise," Jessica called

out from somewhere near Vini. When they hung up, Dani sat there for a moment, looking at the phone. Her smile slowly waned but she quickly schooled her face into a mask of indifference when she heard the front door open, and Ava call out a greeting.

"I'm in the living room."

Ava hustled in and when she saw the phone in Dani's hand, she gestured toward it. "Damn it. Did I miss Vini?"

Dani nodded. "Yeah. It was a really quick call since they were about to head out of town. We could try calling her back?"

Ava shook her head. "I have to change and head out to meet Grace over at Terry's. We joined that new bowling league he started, and the first practice is today. I'll give Vini a quick call later."

"Sounds good. Do you want to go see a movie or something after your bowling practice?"

"I wish I could, but Grace and I are headed up to Atlanta to catch a show. Rain check for when we get back?"

Dani nodded, pasting a smile on her face. "Sounds good. You guys drive carefully and let me know when you get there."

Ava nodded before rushing up the stairs. Dani watched her go and then sighed. It seemed like it would be another quiet weekend for her and whichever streaming service caught her attention first, unless Jordan wanted to get out and about. As if he heard his name in her mind, there was a rumble on the stairs before Jordan came skidding into view.

"Where's the fire, kid?" Dani asked, laughing when he nearly slipped. "Also, what did I tell you about running with only socks on in the house? If you fall and bust your behind, we're not going to the hospital. Just because we have health insurance doesn't mean I'm trying to use it."

Jordan flailed a little, shaking his head at her words. "I'm not running. I'm just walking quickly." Dani hummed, unconvinced, as he continued. "I wanted to see if I could have a sleepover at Nick's. His mom said it was okay."

Dani frowned. "I didn't get a message from her." No sooner had the words left her mouth then her phone dinged. She looked down and saw Nick's mother's name flash on the screen. "Never mind."

"So, can I go?" Jordan sounded so eager. It made sense. Nick was his best friend and had been since they were practically in diapers. His mom, Denise, was from Peach Blossom and though they were a few years apart, she and Dani had gone to the same high school.

Dani narrowed her eyes. "Did you finish all your homework?"

Jordan nodded so fast he looked like one of those bobbleheads people used to have in their cars. "I even cleaned my room."

That had Dani raising her eyebrows. "Wow. You must really want to go to this sleepover. What's so special about it that you plan on abandoning your dear mother for the night?"

He bounced up and down, nearly making Dani nauseous. She could tell he was excited and as much as it pained her, it brought a smile to her face. Jordan had been so quiet right after she and his father, Jacob, had split a few years ago. Maybe she had been bending a little too much one way to make up for it, but Jordan was a good kid, and he never made her regret it.

"I'm not abandoning you," he said rolling his eyes. "But Nick just got this new game that we've all been waiting for so we can get on it and game together. So, can I go? Please?"

He clasped his hands together and gave her a wide smile. Even if she wanted to say no, she wouldn't have been able to resist that face. She was a sucker, and they all knew it. "Fine. Go pack your bag."

"Already done." Jordan scrambled around the couch and pulled out a duffel bag that was clearly ready to go. Dani snorted and shook her head. Clearly, Jordan already knew what she was going to say. Asking was merely a formality. Ava came thumping down the steps then and Dani called out to her.

"Hey, sis. You mind dropping Jordan off at Nick's? Apparently, they're having a boys' night, and I'm not invited."

Ava laughed before gesturing to Jordan. "Yeah. I'll open the door and let him roll out on my way to Grace's. Let's go, kid."

Five minutes later and Dani once again found herself alone. This was quickly becoming a habit, and one she wasn't sure she liked. Still, there wasn't much she could do outside of finding her own hobby. Right then, she remembered Zoey's offer.

The book club.

They only met once a week, but once was better than not at all. At least it would get Dani off the couch and around some people again. She might even find some new favorite authors out of the deal. At least she wouldn't be sitting at home bored. Before she could second-guess herself, she reached for her cell. She had already saved Zoey's number and she brought it up and hit Call.

Waiting for the other woman to pick up was the longest ten seconds of Dani's life. Hopefully, the invitation wasn't rescinded. Dani didn't know if they had a cap on the number of people that could join, or even who else had been invited, but when the call connected and she heard Zoey's sweet voice on the other end of the line, it didn't matter.

"Hey, Zoey. It's Dani. So, about the book club..."

Four

Zoey hung up the phone and stared down at it in silence. She wasn't sure what to make of the past couple minutes. As juvenile as it sounded, it was like Christmas and her birthday had rolled into one to give her an amazing present in the form of a tall, leggy fantasy named Dani. Fingers snapped in front of her face, jolting her from her thoughts.

"What? Why did you snap at me?"

Tiffany stood in front of her, hands on her hips as she gave Zoey a curious look. "Because you were just standing there, staring at your phone," she explained. "What's going on? Was it your brother?"

"No, it wasn't Mason. That was Dani," Zoey said as she slowly shook her head, trying to make sense of her thoughts. It was like as soon as Dani's voice had come over the line, her brain had made an immediate exit, and she was left with nothing more than air between her ears.

She had barely been able to stammer out a greeting before realizing Dani was taking her up on her offer. "She said she wants to join us for the next book club."

Tiffany stared at her for a moment before letting out a loud shout. Zoey instinctually shushed her before looking around and giving the few patrons around them an awkward smile.

"I can't believe I just had to shush you," Zoey joked with a pleased smile. "How are you a librarian and breaking one of our most sacred rules?" She wasn't really angry. She was ridiculously happy at not only the fact that in a few days' time, Dani would be sitting on her couch as they discussed books, but also that Tiffany was clearly just as excited as her about the newest development.

"Who cares," Tiffany aggressively whispered, leaning in to Zoey's space. "This is your time. This is where you and the sexy single mama have your big meet-cute moment that's in every romance novel ever."

She shook her head, but her smile didn't wane. "I don't think it really counts as a meet-cute if we've already met one another. And besides, she's not coming as a date. She's just coming as an acquaintance who is interested in books."

Tiffany waved her hand, dismissing the words. "I refuse to believe this is anything other than romantic overtures, and your pessimism will not change that."

"It's not pessimism," Zoey countered. "It's realism. I don't even know if she would be interested in someone like me. Besides, what are the odds that all of the sisters like women?"

"What are the odds that all of them are straight? What are the odds that all of them are right-handed? Who cares about odds. Your crush is coming to your book club. Why am I more excited than you are?" Was Tiffany more excited than Zoey? That was a good question, and one Zoey didn't have an answer for. She was ridiculously excited to have Dani in her space, but she was also nervous. "And what the hell do you mean 'someone like me'?"

Despite working with the general public, Zoey knew she was not what was considered a people person. She was awkward, and sometimes when she got too excited her brain and her mouth did not always agree on what should and shouldn't be said. It was part of why she started writing. It was easier for her to get words on a page and use them to make sense of the world and how she was feeling than to think of what to say on the fly. Her high school English teacher had encouraged her to share her words, and that plus Mason's never-wavering belief in her led to her writing her first book. Still, two book deals and four novels later, she still felt the grips of imposter syndrome that left her insecure about the viability of her author career.

"I mean, she's in the medical field and has a kid and a house. She has her whole life figured out, and I'm still trying to decide if I'll be here in a year or if I'll end up crashing on my brother's couch and trying to restart again in a new city."

"Well, first of all, I'm not letting you leave," Tiffany said firmly. "Do you know how many librarians we've gone through in the past three years alone? You reaching out to me and agreeing to give my little hometown a shot was a miracle. I'm not letting you get away from me that easily."

Zoey had known that Tiffany was excited when she had agreed to move to Peach Blossom even if the contract was initially just for a year. Zoey had been doing all she could to breathe new life into the little library that had become like home to her. It wasn't like she wanted to leave after a year, but libraries depended on budgets, and this one might not have enough in it to keep her.

"It's not like I want to leave—" Zoey's words were cut off by Tiffany raising her hand, halting the conversation.

"No. We aren't talking about that shit right now. We will save that for another night when you aren't about to be face-to-face again with the future Mrs. Zoey. Right now, I want to understand why you aren't excited about Dani coming to book club."

That had Zoey's heart beating overtime. She had invited Dani to book club on a whim partly because she wanted more time to get to know her, but also because Dani seemed to need something. Zoey had always been observant, and with those skills came her strange ability to guess what people were looking for, particularly when they asked questions in the library. Most of the time it was just about books and their reading habits. Other times it was about activities that the library and surrounding community provided that she helped connect people to. When she and Dani had talked, she had sensed not only that Dani loved books, but that she would enjoy having other people to talk about those books with. And selfishly, Zoey wanted to be there to see Dani's enjoyment.

It wasn't the first book club Zoey had ever established, but it was one of the most surprising ones. When she had put the flier out about establishing the club, she had assumed it would take a while to catch on, but the ten spots she'd had open were immediately filled by the end of the day. She was pleasantly surprised to see that they had a good range of ages too. When the votes for their first book were done, Zoey's shock continued when Mrs. Pauline, one of the older members, had suggested and voted for a book with content warnings that looked like a grocery list. It wasn't chosen, but Zoey had picked it up for herself anyway. For research purposes, of course. Now, she was excited to open it up once again to see how Dani would fit into their group.

"I am excited," Zoey reiterated finally. "I'm just nervous, I guess. What if I say the wrong thing and she gets the wrong impression of me? It's not like we've ever really had an extensive conversation."

Tiffany nodded as she gazed at Zoey. "You have a point," she conceded. "I can understand being so nervous that you might say something that doesn't land as well. But I have no such concerns, so how about I help you out and ask the hard questions?"

"Would you really?" Zoey asked, some of her anxiety melting away. One of the reasons why she and Tiffany worked so well together was because Tiffany was far more outgoing. She didn't seem to agonize about whether or not to say something, like Zoey often did. Sometimes that created awkward situations, but Tiffany always seemed to power through them, emerging on the other side with smiles on her face and the faces of whoever she was talking to. If she ever dwelled on the interactions later, Zoey never knew. Zoey knew that if she had that uncanny ability, she would probably be a menace. It was a good thing that they balanced each other out in that regard.

"Of course," Tiffany said with the smile. "Plus, this way I get to see you and Dani interact, and I can let you know if you should kick things up a notch or dial it back."

Zoey sighed in relief before another thought struck her. She narrowed her eyes and gave Tiffany a considering look. "Do you want to be there just so that you have something to gossip about later on?"

Tiffany noted. "Oh, of course. When you guys are at your wedding, I will be giving the speech about how all this came about. Don't worry, I won't gossip with others. I selfishly want to be the only one who knows how all of this started. Consider it my fee."

Zoey chuckled and shook her head. She would happily pay that fee for Tiffany's help, so she let it go.

"Now that that's settled," Tiffany said, drawing Zoey's attention again. "We need to figure out what you're going to wear for the next book club and which restaurant you're going to recommend."

Zoey frowned. What did a restaurant have to do with anything? "Why do I need to recommend a restaurant?"

"For when you ask her on a date. You need to already have a place in mind to take her. Don't just leave it open-ended. Take initiative. Women like that sort of thing, or so I've been told."

The book in Zoey's hand dropped onto the floor with a loud thump. She hadn't gotten that far in her thoughts. "Date?" she asked, her voice going high. "I can't ask her on a date at book club."

"Why the hell not? Isn't that what all this is for?"

"I mean, yeah," Zoey confirmed. "But after her asking me for help, wouldn't asking her out just seem opportunistic? Like I only asked her over for one thing?"

Tiffany rolled her eyes. "That sounds like a load of bullshit to me. It's not like as soon as she comes in, you're going to invite her to see your strap collection."

"Tiffany," Zoey hissed, reaching out and covering her mouth. She glanced around to see if anyone was paying them attention, and was relieved to see everyone else focused on their books or screens. "I swear, you're going to be the death of me." Zoey slid her hand away and rolled her own eyes at Tiffany's shit-eating grin.

"I'm delightful and you know it," she joked before pushing Zoey with her shoulder. When Zoey sighed, Tiffany patted her on the shoulder. "Cheer up, friend. Leave Operation You Get the Girl to me."

Zoey clearly wasn't thinking straight. She couldn't do this. She had spent the better part of the afternoon brooding over her decision to extend the book club invite to Dani. It wasn't that she didn't want the other woman to come, because she really did. Not just for selfish reasons either. Everyone who came to book club had such varied opinions and it made their insights about whatever book was chosen that month even better. Sometimes, people could be looking at the same situation but have radically different interpretations, colored by their own experiences. The discussions that arose from those differences were what Zoey lived for.

"Oh my gosh, sit down. I don't even like the woman and yet you're making me nervous."

Zoey sighed but did as Tiffany asked, sitting at one of the barstools and trying not to vibrate out of her skin. "Sorry. It's just been a while since…you know. I invited someone over I actually liked."

"Really? I couldn't tell at all," Tiffany joked. She smiled over her shoulder. "Just relax. You had just about everything prepared before I got here. You even dusted your bookshelf."

"I was stress cleaning."

"There's no reason to be stressed out," Tiffany countered. "Dani is going to get here and when your eyes meet over the book, wedding bells will ring, pages will flutter and panties will fly."

Zoey sputtered out a laugh. "Tiffany. You can't just say stuff like that."

Tiffany turned around from the stove and fixed a wicked smile on her face. "And why not? I know that's what you're hoping will happen. I'm just speaking it into the universe to manifest its existence."

Zoey shook her head, but the ridiculous words had done their job. She was feeling a lot more relaxed about the whole thing. By the time the doorbell rang, she was almost calm about the fact that soon enough, Dani would be in her house.

Five

Dani felt like throwing up. She had almost texted Zoey back twice to say she either changed her mind and wasn't coming, or something had come up and she couldn't go. It was for those reasons she knew she needed to fight through the anxiety of doing something new and show up. She couldn't keep hanging around the house alone. She might go crazy if she continued to stare at the same four silent walls. Everyone in the house had more of a social life than her, including Jordan. It was time for Dani to get her shit together and find a little more happiness in her day. If that meant feeling a little awkward about meeting brand-new people, then so be it.

Zoey had told her not to bring anything, that the snacks and drinks would be taken care of, but Dani would have felt weird walking in with nothing in her hands. She hadn't reached back out to see if anyone had allergies, so she hoped a peach cobbler would be neutral enough to be okay.

"Where you headed, kiddo?"

Dani was startled to hear her dad's—Daniel's—voice as she was walking out the door. He was getting out of his car with a couple of plastic bags. She lifted the cobbler dish in her hand. "Headed to Zoey's for a book club meeting." She paused. "Did you need me for anything?"

Daniel shook his head. "Nah. You go on and have fun with your club. I'm going to make me some food and settle in for a quiet night at home."

Dani kissed him on the cheek when he leaned down before continuing to her car. She made sure the cobbler dish was secure before throwing the car in Reverse and making her way to Zoey's. It didn't take long. They only lived a couple roads apart, but even though it was a short ride, she still found time to let her anxiety grow. She should have asked more questions about who was going to be there. It wouldn't have changed her mind about making an appearance, but at least she would have been able to know who else was there ahead of time. All Zoey had mentioned was that there were about nine people— well, ten now, including Dani. She wasn't sure if that was a normal number for a book club or not.

The sky was painted in light purples as she turned on to Zoey's street. The duplex she was in had once been a large single-family home. That's what most homes were in Peach Blossom. The town only had one apartment complex, with a couple others twenty to thirty minutes away. Dani knew it was the old librarian's home that Zoey was renting. The older woman had retired and promptly made her way to Florida to be with her daughter and grandchildren. Dani could understand wanting to be with them now that she had more free time. Dani's dad had been the same way when he had retired, filling in for Dani in as many school activities for Jordan as possible.

When Dani pulled into the driveway, she had to pause for a moment to compose herself. She wasn't sure why she was feeling so unsettled. It's not like she didn't deal with people all day. She was a nurse. Dealing with people was part of her job, and that included people she wasn't close to. But after her mom's death so many years ago, the Williams clan had grown very close and tended to stick together. Having two other sisters meant that Dani had built-in friends even as much as they bickered and argued. It was always sort of them against the world.

Now, with Ava and Grace practically joined at the hip, and Vini becoming a world traveler with Jessica, Dani was finding herself having to make new friends again for the first time in decades. She wasn't even sure if she was good at it anymore. It's not like she didn't have friends outside of her sisters, but the past few years she had been busy with helping Vini keep the family business, getting divorced and concentrating on raising Jordan. Having all that change left her realizing she had been neglecting herself in many ways, leaving her slightly adrift now that the realization had bubbled to the surface.

"Maybe this will be good for me," she said to herself. There was no one else around to confirm or deny that statement. It was becoming a familiar scene, and one she was quickly growing tired of, so she sighed before moving to get out of the of the car. She didn't want to make it weird by being seen pulling up and just sitting in her parked car outside of Zoey's house. She grabbed the cobbler and walked to the front door. When she knocked, she could hear muffled voices that continued even after the door was opened.

"Just in time." Dani smiled and nodded at Tiffany. She recognized the other librarian from the many times she had come in. They hadn't really talked, given that Zoey was the one in charge of the esports club Jordan was in, but Tiffany was from Peach Blossom, which meant Dani knew of her.

"Hey, Tiffany," Dani said in greeting before holding up the dessert dish. "I brought a cobbler. I know Zoey said not to bring anything, but it would feel weird if I showed up empty-handed when I don't even have the book."

Tiffany giggled before reaching out and taking the cobbler dish. "No way, this is perfect. I remember you bringing a cobbler in for us once before."

Dani nodded and walked through the doorway when Tiffany gestured for her to come in. She closed the door behind her, glad for a small moment to prepare herself for being social for the night. "I did. It was during that library potluck you guys had a couple months ago. I think you were raising funds for new laptops or computers or something."

"That's right. There was so much good food brought in, but I still remember that cobbler. We were sad when there wasn't any left to pilfer, so you bringing us one now is more than perfect," Tiffany said. She led Dani back through the formal living room and into the kitchen.

There, Dani tried not to let her nerves get the best of her when the conversation that had been going on died down and seven other pairs of eyes turned to look at her. It was a lot like walking into the classroom on her first day of school. She recognized some of the faces, given that Peach Blossom was a small town, but when she saw Zoey sitting there with a little smile on her face, Dani felt a profound sense of relief.

Zoey was in that mustard-yellow cardigan that on anyone else would have looked awkward, but on her looked perfect and pillow soft. Large square-shaped black frames fit her face perfectly, and her curly hair was like a soft halo around her heart-shaped face.

"Hey, Zoey. Thanks for inviting me."

Zoey stood up quickly and walked over to Dani. "I'm so glad you came." She looked down at the dish in Tiffany's hand. "Oh, you didn't have to bring anything. I made snacks and got drinks for everyone."

Dani shrugged. "I know, but I wanted to bring something. It's the first time I've ever been to your place, so consider it a housewarming present or a thank-you for inviting me to book club. It's nice to get out of the house every now and then, and if it's about books, it's even better." Zoey looked back up at her with a wide smile, and Dani tried to ignore the way her breath caught.

"I agree," Zoey said. "I know it's probably a little bit

of a stereotype to be a librarian and start a book club, but I couldn't resist. Tiffany and I tended to chat about books that we were reading anyway, so starting a book club just seemed so perfect."

"It is perfect," Dani said. She could almost taste Zoey's excitement. It was invigorating to have someone enjoy their work so much. Not everyone could say that, but with Zoey, it was evident in the way she talked and the way her hands almost fluttered with the words, as if trying to take flight. When a throat cleared, Dani blinked quickly and realized that she was standing there, staring at Zoey even after the other women had stopped talking. Zoey seemed to realize the same thing, and she took a step back before turning and gesturing to the rest of the group.

"Well, how about we do some introductions to reacquaint everyone. We have a couple new people, so you aren't the only one, Dani."

Zoey delivered that line with a smile, but rather than be relieved, Dani felt a little down. She had thought she was the only one who had just received an invite, but of course there were others who Zoey probably reached out to. She was just being friendly. And why was Dani feeling some type of way about it anyway? She pushed the thought from her mind as Zoey called everyone over to grab some food, and it wasn't until they were settled into seats in the den that Dani realized she didn't know how to start conversations with anyone. It wasn't that she didn't know them, she just didn't know them well enough to know what to talk about. Thankfully, Tiffany decided to jump in and get things started.

"So, since we have some new faces," she started, drawing everyone's attention. "I thought it would be great to start with a little icebreaker to kick things off. Why don't we go around and tell one interesting fact about ourselves."

Everyone nodded their heads, and Dani verbally agreed as well. She wasn't sure what to really say. There wasn't anything interesting about her. She was a nurse, and she had a kid. That was the extent of her life right now.

"I see some hesitation, so why don't I start." Tiffany put her plate down and sat up, looking around the group. "My name is Tiffany. I foster feral kittens, and I am bisexual."

Dani smiled and clapped politely along with the group. She tried to pay attention when the next person said their piece as well. When it finally came to her, she blurted out the only thing she could think of.

"I'm Dani, and I am going through a quarter-life crisis." She gripped her glass tightly, not sure what to expect after her proclamation, but when she saw some nods and smiles, her shoulders relaxed just a bit.

One of the other women, Sharon, spoke up. "It's like that sometimes. When my son moved out for college, I thought for sure I was going to throw a party and enjoy my next phase of life. I am enjoying it, but damn if I didn't have to reevaluate who I was. Hang in there, girl."

"Same with me," another woman chimed in. "When my daughter, Becky, started high school, all she wanted to do was talk on that dang phone with her friends. I swear she's going to have a hump on her back from leaning over the damn thing so much."

Dani smiled and lifted a glass. She did feel a little better about divulging things to people who seemed to understand, even if they were just acquaintances she would only see once a week. When she caught Zoey's eye, Dani smiled. The warm grin she got back loosened something in her chest, and Dani was surprised when she relaxed further. Their gazes locked for a few more moments before Zoey turned and spoke up.

"Well, of course you know me. I'm Zoey and the co-founder of book club. And I have a brother in the army who recently came back from living overseas."

That was news to Dani. She didn't know a lot about Zoey outside of what Jordan usually divulged, though his words were usually about something video game related. "I didn't know you had a brother," she said. "That must be hard on your parents, having him overseas." When she saw a couple people wince, she wondered what she had said wrong. Even Tiffany's normally wide smile dimmed slightly.

"Well, it probably would be, but they're dead so I'm sure it's fine."

Well, fuck. Now Dani knew why some of the others had made those faces. She had royally put her foot in it.

"Oh shit, I'm sorry about that. I shouldn't have said—"

Zoey shook her head, halting her words. "No, it's fine. You didn't know, and it's not something I just casually sprinkle into conversations when people are asking about book recommendations." Zoey reached out and touched Dani's arm. The palm of her hand was warmer and softer that Dani thought it would be. "They died a long time ago. It's just my brother and me now. He raised me since there wasn't really anyone else to do it."

"Still," Dani started, thoroughly chagrined. "I shouldn't have just assumed."

"The thing is, I sort of have a family as is. And it's a family I get to choose," Zoey said with an open smile. "Found families are kind of the best as evidenced by this month's book."

Dani appreciated the segue into a new topic. Her gaze was on Zoey as she stood up and walked over to an absolutely massive wall of books. Her eyes widened as she took in all the titles.

"I know," Zoey said, pulling her attention. "How many books does one girl truly need, right? I just can't help myself sometimes. But the good thing about being a book collector—"

"Hoarder."

"—is," Zoey continued, ignoring Tiffany's comment, "I usually have excellent book recommendations, and I always have a book you can borrow." She slid a book from the bookshelf before walking over and handing it to Dani.

Dani reached up to take the book from Zoey, and for a moment their gazes met again. Dani couldn't help but note just how pretty Zoey was. She wasn't lying before when she said that Zoey's glasses were cute and perfectly fit her face. Even from behind lenses, Zoey's dark brown eyes drew Dani in. When their fingers brushed, it was like touching a bit of lightning, sharp and invigorating. Dani had never really felt that sensation before, and she wasn't sure what to make of it. When she reluctantly pulled her hand away, she realized that her cheeks were warm. It was something she had only experienced a handful of times before, and with a jolt she realized what that could mean.

"Thanks," Dani said, trying to keep her voice as calm as normal. "How much do I owe you for it?"

Zoey took a step back as if just realizing they were not alone. She shook her head.

"Don't worry about it. Consider it a 'welcome to book club' gift."

Dani swallowed hard before covering up her reaction with a smirk. "Some people buy flowers. Librarians buy books. Noted." When Zoey dropped her head, smile still visible, Dani couldn't help but chuckle at how damn cute she was. Maybe coming to book club was a good idea after all.

Six

"Hey, you. Long time no see."

Dani looked up when her coworker Natasha walked over to the nurses' desk. "Hey, stranger," Dani replied with a smile that had been etched on her face for the past three days since book club. "It's been a while since you darkened these halls. How was your vacation?"

Natasha flopped down in the chair beside Dani with a groan. "It was so perfect that being back here automatically depresses me. I'm regretting not finding a sugar daddy so I could have made it a permanent thing."

"Wouldn't you have to put out for that?"

"Not necessarily," Natasha answered before lifting her head and spearing Dani with a searching look. "You seem different. Did something happen while I was gone?"

Dani raised her eyebrows. "What do you mean?" She looked down at herself but couldn't see anything different about herself. "Everything is the same as before."

Natasha shook her head. "Nah. You're smiling way too hard. Who did you sleep with?"

Dani moved to cover Natasha's mouth before looking around. They couldn't leave the nurses' desk right now, but she didn't want to have other people overhearing the conversation and getting curious. Small towns were notorious for letting rumors get more than a little out of hand before they could be reined back in.

"I haven't slept with anyone," Dani insisted. She knew she was smiling a little more than she had been before, but she hadn't realized her giddiness was that noticeable. "I just joined a book club. That's the only thing that changed since you've been gone. It's nothing serious."

"Then why are you cheesing so hard?" Natasha insisted. She leaned closer to Dani. "Are you reading something really smutty?"

Dani laughed and shook her head. The book they were reading was good, but it hadn't been particularly spicy so far. "No. It's good though. I can't remember whose choice it was, but they chose very well."

Natasha eyed her for a moment longer before she conceded. "Fine. I assumed from that grin on your face that either the ex-husband had showed up to do his job as a co-parent, or you had done some leg spreading, not page spreading, but as long as you're happy."

Dani chuckled at that, shaking her head at Natasha's antics. "Really? The whole 'if you like it, I love it' angle?"

Natasha shrugged. "Not that I don't have books I enjoy,

but damn, I thought you were putting yourself back out there."

"I am," Dani insisted. "I went to a book club. That's the definition of putting myself out there."

"Not like that," Natasha countered with a roll of her eyes. "You know I meant putting yourself out there when it comes to dating, not these one-off social clubs or whatever. Are there any single men at book club at least? I know the last guy you went out with didn't click, but that doesn't mean you should give up now."

Dani swallowed hard before turning back to the computer in front of her. She had been in the middle of inputting patient information, but the words on the screen might as well have been Klingon. None of them made sense in the face of her rolling thoughts. There had been a vague inkling on the edge of her mind for days.

"Why do you assume I…" Her voice trailed off as she tried to decide whether or not to finish her sentence. Saying it made it so much more real, and she wasn't quite sure if she was there yet. Could she take the words back once they were already out there? Were there rules against that? "Maybe I don't need to date right now. Maybe what I need is to get out and be social so I can remember how to do that before I add romance to the mix."

"Well, what about the last guy you dated? What exactly happened with that one? You only gave me vague information over text that you didn't click, but what exactly was the reason?"

Dani shrugged, which perfectly summed up how she

felt about that date; the last few dates really. The guy had been nice, but there was nothing there. There were no sparks—hell, there weren't even small pops. The most exciting thing had been the food, leaving Dani feeling equal parts guilty and frustrated. Had her divorce really messed her up that badly to where she couldn't even go on a normal date and feel anything at all? When had she last felt something for someone?

As soon as she thought of that question, a memory surfaced of easy smiles and the brush of hands as a book passed between them. Dani was surprised at how easily her mind conjured up the image, and even more surprised at how she could almost feel the whisper of that touch even now. There was nothing even remotely sexual about the brush of hands and yet here she was, thoughts lingering on it days later. When she realized she had been staring into space, Dani quickly shook herself out of it and answered Natasha's question.

"The date was fine. He was a very nice guy."

"But," Natasha prompted.

Dani shrugged again, not knowing exactly how to explain it. "But I didn't feel a connection with him. He was nice and that was just it."

Natasha nodded with a considering look. Dani waited patiently, turning back to the computer and inputting more information. She liked talking to Natasha about things like this because she wasn't impulsive with her words. Sure, she liked to run off at the mouth like they all did, but Dani knew when it got down to it, Natasha always thought carefully about what she wanted to say, and so those words carried weight.

"Maybe you need something or someone different to shake things up," Natasha said finally. "You've only dated people from Peach Blossom, people you've known for years, so maybe everything just seems too one-tone for you."

Dani pursed her lips, considering it. Natasha wasn't wrong. Dani's ex-husband had been a classmate from high school, and everyone else she had sporadically dated over the years was from the same relatively small social circle. Dani wasn't interested in leaving Peach Blossom. It wasn't just because she was from here, but also her family was here. Jordan had strong, stable friendships cultivated almost since birth, and the town was safe not only for him, but also for Ava and Vini. Dani loved the small-town comforts, and Peach Blossom took it a step further by being welcoming to most everyone who set foot in town. She doubted she would find that anywhere else, so she had never really considered branching too far out and dating someone from a city too far away. She also had never been that interested in online dating, so that left her with a lot of time and very few people to spend it with.

"What about this," Natasha said, drawing Dani's attention again. "I have a friend who lives about an hour away in Tulipsville. I know you aren't interested in moving, but an hour isn't so bad and he's not even originally from there."

"I don't know, Tash," Dani replied slowly. She wasn't

sure if she even wanted to jump into another date when the last ones hadn't been great to begin with. Then again, maybe that was her problem. She hadn't been all in on those dates to begin with. Maybe she just needed an attitude adjustment. "I mean...what if it doesn't go any better?"

"Then you shrug it off and keep it moving," Natasha said firmly. Dani hoped some of her confidence would rub off on Dani. She wasn't feeling apprehensive about the whole thing. She was just tired. Something in her was beginning to wonder if maybe the problem wasn't that she was trying, but that she shouldn't be. Maybe she wasn't meant to be with someone. It was a thought that had been circling the drain of her mind lately. She knew the famous line about there being someone for everyone, but she was really beginning to think that was crap.

Dani really wanted to say no, but Natasha looked so earnestly sure that she gave in. Besides, it was just one date. If sparks didn't fly, then she would at least get a meal out of it that she didn't have to cook herself, and spend some time with another adult for a couple hours. If sparks did fly, then maybe her lingering memories of how it felt to brush fingers with Zoey was just a fluke. She wasn't sure which way she wanted things to go.

"Fine. I'll go on a date with him," Dani replied finally. She smiled at Natasha's soft noise of excitement and let a little of that bleed into her own feelings. "But only if you're sure he's not the type to get bent out of shape if I say thanks but no thanks."

Natasha held a hand up and put her other over her heart. "Scout's honor he's a good guy. I wouldn't be friends with someone who was going to be a dick about rejection, let alone introduce him to one of my friends."

Dani shrugged. "Just had to check. You never know these days." When Natasha nodded in agreement, Dani felt a little better about saying yes. There was still some anxiety like normal when she thought of going on dates, but she was firmly reserving judgement. "Feel free to give him my number."

Natasha smiled wide and nodded. "I will. You're going to like him. I can feel it."

Dani didn't feel much of anything at the moment, but she chalked it up to being at work and tried to push the upcoming date from her mind.

Seven

Zoey didn't get off work often. She worked a normal shift at the library, but because it was often understaffed with no room in the budget to hire another employee, she often took advantage of the overtime by filling in where she was needed. Today was different. The library was slow enough that another hand wasn't needed, which gave Zoey time to explore the town at her leisure. Her latest book proposal had been accepted, which hadn't been a surprise since it had been part of the discussions for her last release. What had been a surprise was how quickly the publisher had agreed, given the book was a new genre for her.

Zoey had been toying with the idea of a cozy murder mystery set in a small town, but she had never really lived in one. When she had talked to Tiffany about the idea, she was quick to tell Zoey to come to Peach Blossom. The head librarian there had been holding off on retirement until they found someone to fill the empty librarian slot. With Zoey's interest, the woman had jumped at it and Zoey had quickly put in for the position, seeing it as killing two birds with one stone when it came to finding a small town to help with research and catching up with her friend. She had been even more shocked at how excited her agent and editor were when she mentioned her book being based off the town she was currently calling home for at least the next year.

It was her first book set in a small town, and while she was excited, she was also slightly apprehensive. This was going to take a bit more additional research, considering she had lived either on base when she was a child and moved around based on her older brother's deployment schedule, or in a big city when she had moved for college. Small town life had always appealed to her, with the camaraderie that came with being familiar down to the very bones of your generation. She had wanted to taste what that was like since she was a child and felt almost lost in the shuffle of military life. She was grateful that not only was her brother able to get guardianship of her, but that he was actually willing to take care of her in the first place. It helped that they were only eight years apart, but he was still young when she moved with him. Mason did the best he could, but there were times when Zoey felt like she missed out on a lot of things that went with having a nuclear family.

The problem Zoey found herself in now is that she hadn't actually started writing her book yet. She usually preferred to do as much research as possible before she penned her first word, but she had a firm deadline for this first draft, and she had been staring at a blank document for several weeks with no clue where to start. She had an idea of the characters she wanted to incorporate, but she needed more. That's how she found herself strolling through downtown Peach Blossom, waving at the few familiar faces that walked by. Zoey recognized mostly the children who tended to come in for the library's children's reading time twice a week, as well as a few of the parents who stayed around enjoying the quiet that came with someone else tending to their kids for an hour. She didn't doubt that for some, that was the only quiet time they got outside of bedtime or if the kids were at school.

Unable to help herself, Zoey stopped in the bookstore. Just because she was a librarian didn't mean she got to check out books whenever she wanted. Plus, she still had to return them when she did. The many books in her living room were a collection of either books she had received from fellow authors and publishers, or those she had purchased herself. She had a book budget, and with a sigh, she noted that she was already long past it for the month.

"Hey, Zoey. Back to grab a few more books today?" Ellie called out. Zoey smiled but shook her head as Ellie walked around one of the aisles. Her smile was wide, and she was carrying a stack of books in her hands. Zoey was curious, but she knew if she let herself get distracted with other people's books, she would never finish writing her own.

"Not today. I think you obliterated my book budget for the next few months," Zoey said with a smile. She didn't mind going over budget every now and then when the new releases were so hard to ignore, but she tried not to make it a habit. "Just wandering a bit to get some inspiration." Ellie knew Zoey was an author. It wasn't like Zoey was trying to keep it like some firmly guarded secret. It just didn't usually come up in everyday conversation.

"Awesome. Let me know if you need a beta reader when you're done. I'd love to read more of your work."

Zoey knew Ellie was serious and not just blowing smoke up her ass. It was nice to be able to talk books with someone else, especially someone who had a girlfriend who was also a creative. Ellie had let it slip that her girlfriend, Nova, was a singer, and was surprised when Zoey had a small freak-out moment. Some of Nova's songs had been stars of Zoey's book playlists, especially because her last album was explicitly about women loving other women. Ellie had been so bashful when Zoey mentioned it that she had immediately known Ellie was the muse that had served as inspiration.

"I definitely will," Zoey replied as she made her way out of the store before her wallet accidentally fell open and money spilled out in exchange for books she didn't need.

From the bookstore, she finally decided to make her way to the bowling alley. She had talked to Terry a couple days ago about speaking with him about his family's deep roots in Peach Blossom. From what little she had found in her own research, his family was one of the founding families that essentially built Peach Blossom from the ground up. Those were the type of deep roots she needed to explore because as someone who had never even been back to visit the city she was born in, it seemed almost improbable to Zoey for multiple generations to continue to live in one place even as the decades rolled by.

Zoey wiped the sweat from her brow. It was still spring, but summer was not far away, and she was regretting choosing to walk instead of drive. When she opened the door to the bowling alley, Zoey let out a sigh of relief as cool air rushed toward her. She was so deep in her enjoyment of central air-conditioning that she almost ran straight into someone exiting the alley at the same time.

"Oh, excuse me," Zoey said, taking a step to the side.

"You're fine. Wait, aren't you Zoey?"

It took a moment for Zoey's eyes to acclimate to the dimmer light, but once they had, she blinked quickly, trying to remember where she had seen the two women in front of her. "Yes?"

The other woman smiled and at once she looked even more familiar. "I've seen you a couple times when I came to pick Jordan up when Dani had to work. I'm her sister, Ava."

Zoey widened her eyes all at once, understanding why the other woman looked familiar and yet not. She vaguely remembered seeing her at the library, but it was mostly her similarity to Dani that helped put the pieces together.

"Oh, nice to meet you. Sorry for almost bowling you over."

The other woman standing beside her smiled and Zoey was damn near blinded by how perfect her smile was. The woman was taller than Ava by a few inches, with the type of skin that looked like smooth butter and a style that was the perfect blend of feminine and masculine. Zoey felt downright dumpy by comparison with her faded blue T-shirt and boyfriend jeans.

"I'm Grace," the woman said before holding her hand out. Zoey scrambled to shake it instead of standing there staring. Dani was most definitely the person she was interested in right now, but Zoey was enamored, not dead. Grace was gorgeous and Ava was cute as hell. If Zoey had known small towns had such cute women, she might have gone to one sooner. "It's nice to finally meet you."

"Yeah, Jordan talks about you all the time," Ava added. She cocked her head to the side. "Dani had mentioned how cute you looked in your new glasses and she wasn't wrong."

Now, Zoey felt her cheeks heat up and she had to fight hard not to bring her hands up to cup them. It wasn't the first time she had been called cute, but it was still tough to get used to after having been such an awkward kid. It took her a minute to clock Ava's words, but when she did, she couldn't help but widen her eyes.

"Dani has mentioned me?" Once the words were out there, Zoey couldn't pull them back. She held her breath when Ava gave her a considering look. She knew her words probably gave her away, so she thought quickly to figure out how she could salvage the situation without looking like she desperately wanted to know what else Dani might have said about her. Even though she pretty much did. She was like a black hole starving for any little bit of information about what Dani thought about her. Or if.

"Did she find the books I suggested for her helpful?"

Ava's expression didn't change. "What books?"

"The ones...um, the self-help books." Now Zoey was wondering if she was talking too much. What if Dani didn't want Ava to know about the books? "She asked for some advice. Well, I don't know about 'ask for advice' so much as helpful suggestions. The advice was all me. Hopefully it wasn't too much, and I didn't overstep."

Grace snorted. "Trust me, if you had overstepped with Dani, she would have let you know. She isn't exactly known for biting her tongue." Ava agreed with her, though her shrewd eyes never left Zoey's face. It was unnerving being under that stare. It reminded Zoey of the look Mason always got when he figured out she was lying about something.

"Are you interested in Dani?" Ava asked, her tone too even for Zoey to glean any emotion.

"I...what?" Flustered, Zoey wasn't sure what to say, her tongue tripping up and saying a lot of nothing. Ava didn't elaborate and when Zoey glanced over, Grace didn't even have the decency to look surprised. "Interested how?"

Ava smiled and shrugged. "Platonically. Romantically. Take your pick."

"Oh, well. She's really nice to talk to. And she has great taste in books," Zoey said, trying to figure out a way to salvage the conversation. There was no way any information she gave wouldn't get back to Dani. She looked around, wondering if Dani was here, waiting in the background to pop out and say "Gotcha."

"She's not here if that's what you're worried about," Ava added, as if she had read Zoey's mind. That did make Zoey feel a bit better about the direction of the conversation, but she still wasn't sure how much she should divulge. It was one thing to talk with Tiffany about her helpless crush on Dani, but it was another completely to voice it aloud to other people. Especially if one of those people was Dani's own sister. Plus, Zoey wasn't trying to be one of those lesbians who pined over a straight woman. Not again anyway.

"I wasn't worried," Zoey replied quickly. "I just didn't want to seem like I was talking about her behind her back or anything. Dani just started joining us for book club and I want her to feel comfortable there with me."

Whatever Ava seemed to be looking for, she nodded as if she found it before smiling widely. Instantly the air seemed lighter, and Zoey felt herself able to breathe a little easier. "I'm glad she's found something to enjoy for herself. I've been a little worried about her lately." Ava stepped toward Zoey before placing a hand lightly on her arm. "I don't know what's going on with Dani, but I'm glad she has someone to turn to, even if it's just for book recommendations."

Zoey swallowed hard before nodding once sharply. Ava's smile didn't change, but Zoey felt like she had confirmed something vital. Ava slid past her with a soft goodbye. Grace clapped her on the shoulder with a wide grin.

"Good luck. These Williams sisters are a handful, but definitely worth it."

Zoey watched Grace follow Ava out and tried not to let her heart hope too much at those parting words.

Eight

Dani looked at herself in the mirror before sighing. She wasn't the least bit excited for tonight's date, and yet here she was getting ready, instead of settling down in her comfy pants with a good book and her newest candle. She had told Natasha she would go on the date with her friend Vernon, and she was sure he was just as nice as Natasha said, but she wasn't under any illusion that this might turn into something. Dani had promised to be open, but months—if not years—of going on date after date with nothing more to show than a rather impressive list of restaurants and café spots had left her less than enthused about having to put a bra on and actually leave her house. She would much rather have hunkered down with the book club's book choice of the month.

Thinking about book club led to thinking about Zoey, and Dani had the strangest urge to call her up and ask what she thought about it all. They weren't close enough friends for that, but something about the way Zoey had calmly given her advice a week or so ago left Dani wondering what more Zoey would say if Dani picked her mind.

Why am I thinking about Zoey when I'm supposed to be getting prepared for this damn date. Dani stared at her reflection as if it would reply back and give her the answer she was seeking. If it had been that easy, she would have asked the mirror questions a long time ago, namely what the upcoming winning lottery numbers were and why did the clothes dryer keep eating one of her socks. Questions that were really important. With another deep sigh, Dani gritted her teeth and put on her earrings. Now that they were on, she really had to leave the house. She was making an effort, and she hoped someone appreciated that.

Abruptly, her bedroom door opened, and she heard a soft wolf whistle come from the doorway.

"Look at you looking all fancy. Where are you going?" Ava walked into the room and gave Dani an assessing look. "I don't remember the last time I saw you wear that particular dress. I didn't even know you still owned clothes that weren't scrubs or sweat suits."

Dani glanced at her in the mirror and raised an eyebrow. "Did you forget how to knock, or are you just trying to be annoying?"

Ava rolled her eyes before dropping down on Dani's bed. "I know you're not talking about knocking after barging into my room like two days ago. The only knocking you need to worry about is knocking some boots with whoever the mystery date is."

Dani grimaced. She hadn't met this guy and all she had seen of him a picture from social media. He was good-looking with medium brown skin and dark curly hair. His eyes had looked kind in the photo, and he definitely had a nice smile, yet outside of objectively seeing that he was an attractive person, Dani didn't feel much of anything. He wasn't someone who she would have walked up to on the street, but she had never done that to anyone to begin with.

"That reaction was not what I was expecting," Ava said, pulling Dani's attention back to the conversation at hand. Ava was sitting on her bed, arms crossed and leveling a suspicious look in Dani's direction. It was a look that Dani didn't think she deserved. She was doing what everyone said she should, putting herself out there and trying something and someone new. She was going on dates and giving people a shot, and yet she still just couldn't feel any sense of connection. Hell, she felt more connection with Zoey at book club than she had with any of the people she had gone out with the past few months—if not years.

Dani didn't understand what her problem was. Then again, it was just nice to have a conversation that she was really interested in, especially with people who weren't related to her. Still, maybe she just wasn't meant to have a partner. It wouldn't be completely out of the realm of possibility to never remarry. Her dad hadn't after her mom had passed away, and he seemed totally fine. Then again, he had also been getting out more lately, so Dani knew she needed to do the same.

"I don't know what you want from me," Dani said finally.

"I don't want anything in particular from you. I'm just curious how you're feeling about the date, given your lack of visible enthusiasm."

Dani shrugged. "The reason for that is because I'm not enthused. But I am grateful that you're willing to stay home with Jordan."

"Of course I'll stay home with my nephew," Ava replied easily. "That's not even a question."

"I didn't want to interrupt any plans you had with Grace."

Ava waved her hand like Dani's words were ridiculous enough to not need to be considered. "Grace is having some sort of family intervention over video chat, so I don't want to be anywhere near that. Besides, the nephew and I might head to the library so he can show me what video games the kids are into these days. I'm trying to build a lesson around story building by engaging different and more modern forms of storytelling."

Dani's heartbeat jumped at the thought of the library, or more specifically, who was in the library. "Oh? Tell Zoey I said hi if you see her."

Ava's eyebrow raised. "I saw her earlier today."

"Where? Why didn't you say something about that earlier?"

"Why do you care?"

Dani froze for a split second before purposefully relaxing into a more casual stance.

Ava continued. "Is there something I need to know when it comes to the newest transplant to town?"

Dani scoffed. "No. Just… Zoey is the one who invited me to book club and I'm grateful, since it gets me out of the house for some adult time."

"How adult are we talking? Is this group all about the smut or are we having tantalizing literary conversations?"

It was Dani's time to roll her eyes. "Who says those two things are mutually exclusive?"

"Perfect answer," Ava agreed with a nod. "Put on the gold dangle earrings. They'll go perfectly with that neckline."

Dani nodded before taking off the earrings she had originally put on and doing just that. She smoothed her hands down her dress before turning. "Okay. Finished. How do I look?"

"Amazing. He's going to love you." Ava's smile was genuine, and it raised Dani's spirits enough to get her out the door with a final wave and a shout of goodbye. She still wasn't that excited about the date, but she would fake it until the rest of her finally got on board.

The urge to sigh was high, but Dani forced herself to maintain politeness as the plate in front of her was cleared away. The food had been delicious, and she was already internally adding it to the list of places she wanted to try again later, but other than that, the date had been as unremarkable as always. She had been anxious the entire drive to the restaurant, tapping her fingers against the steering wheel and fighting the desire to jerk into the turning lane, make a U-turn and go back home. That wasn't because of Vernon in its entirety.

When she had walked into the restaurant and been shown to her seat, she had been pleasantly surprised that Vernon's pictures matched who he was in real life. That didn't always happen. There had been a couple times when the photos had either clearly been old or doctored up a bit, but his were true to life. It was a shame really that when they had shaken hands, Dani felt like this was a business dinner rather than a date.

"So, what did you think?" he asked, drawing her attention. The conversation hadn't been stilted or marred by any forced awkwardness. It had just been a bit flat. The type of conversation Dani might have in the grocery checkout line while she waited her turn to scan and pay.

She looked around before answering. "This place is really cute, and the food was great. I'll definitely have to come back to try that salmon dish."

Vernon nodded with a soft smile displaying perfect teeth. His smooth dark skin absorbed the warm glow from the candles on the table and seemed to reflect it back. He was objectively a good-looking man. So why didn't Dani feel anything when looking at him? She wasn't expecting to want to jump his bones immediately or anything. She had never been one to just hop into bed with someone without at least getting to know them a little bit at first. But this just brought her back to her confusion at her lack of interest in anyone she had dated as of late. At first, she thought because they were already familiar to her, but now she was wondering if it was deeper than that. What did all of these guys have in common that just wasn't doing it for her?

"Dani?"

"Yeah?" She blinked quickly and realized Vernon was staring at her with an expectant expression. "Sorry. What was it you were saying?"

He looked at her for a moment before speaking. "I asked if you wanted to get dessert."

"Oh," Dani said, looking down at the tablecloth. Truthfully, she wasn't having a terrible time, but she wasn't sure how much longer she could pretend that this might go anywhere. Maybe a change of scenery would help. "There's a new ice-cream shop about a ten-minute walk from here that's supposed to be good. We could get dessert there?"

Vernon nodded before turning to find their waitress, and it gave Dani time to collect herself. She still needed to figure out what to say to let him down easy and make sure it didn't affect her and Natasha's relationship. She didn't think it would, but it was always a good thing to be cautious. This was also why she didn't like being set up by people she knew. If the relationship put forth went well, then that was all fine and dandy. But if it didn't, then that could lead to unintended consequences that she didn't want to deal with.

The air outside the restaurant was cooler than it had been the past few days. Vernon offered his jacket, but Dani declined. She knew she would warm up with the walk, and she didn't want to lead him into thinking she wanted more.

"So, what are you looking for in a guy?"

It was a good question. Dani could admit that, but it wasn't one that she was prepared to answer, because she still didn't know. Vernon's expression was hopeful, and for a moment she felt bad about not having a suitable response prepared. It wasn't like she hadn't talked about it before, but that was more in the abstract sense. She had never really sat down and listed out the qualities she was looking for in a person beyond the vague approximations that anyone could fit. Clearly that meant something was wrong with her, right? Who goes on dates without a specific idea of the type of person they're looking for in mind?

Her, apparently.

"Oh, I don't know," Dani said finally. Vernon's expression didn't change, and she felt comfortable with continuing. Maybe it would be cathartic to get this out to someone who wasn't a friend or family member. Perhaps Vernon being a total stranger and not familiar with her past to a certain extent would be a good thing. All everyone else really knew was the Dani who had been married, gotten divorced and had been nonstop working hard to make sure she could take care of her kid. But sometimes she thought they forgot that labor was not the be-all and end-all of her personality. Sometimes, she wondered if she had forgotten the same thing.

"I mean," she said, trying again to answer. "I have a kid, so I guess I'm looking for someone who doesn't mind already having a prepackaged family. Maybe someone who compliments me for things other than taking out the trash or cooking a meal." She wasn't trying to sound bitter, but when Dani truly thought about it, she couldn't remember the last time she had been complimented for herself and not for something she had done for someone else.

Vernon nodded. "Well, for what it's worth, I think you look amazing tonight."

Dani looked at him for a moment before laughing. She could appreciate the humor, and it was nice being told she looked good, especially given her usual outfits of scrubs or sweats. For a moment, she wished that was enough to awaken something, anything involving feelings for Vernon. He seemed like a really nice guy, but *nice* just wasn't cutting it for her. She needed something more.

"Well, thank you," she replied, remembering her manners. "I think you look very nice tonight as well."

"But..." Vernon prompted.

Dani huffed out a soft laugh. Vernon was a smart man who obviously knew that she wasn't feeling it. "But I don't know if this date—" Right when they reached the ice-cream shop, the door swung out, nearly clipping her in the shoulder.

Dani jumped back, her eyes widening when it was Zoey who walked out of the ice-cream shop. Dani's gaze slid over her, admiring the light sheen of the curls that framed Zoey's face as well as the yellow cardigan that always looked soft enough to make Dani's fingers itch to touch.

"Hey, Zoey. What a surprise seeing you here." When Zoey looked up, her eyes widened before slowly crawling down Dani's frame. The look had Dani warming up, and she swore a bead of sweat slid down her back between her shoulder blades. How could a look seem so innocent and yet feel so heavy at the same damn time? For a moment, Dani wondered if the dress was too much. When Zoey's gaze fixed back on her own, Dani couldn't read the emotion in it, leaving her feeling off-kilter.

"Dani." Zoey's voice was soft and slightly deeper than it normally sounded. "You look...wow."

The smile that stretched Dani's lips had her cheeks aching. "Really?" When Zoey nodded, Dani felt the strangest urge to twirl. She barely restrained herself and forced her focus on the ice cream in Zoey's hand. "Thank you."

"You're welcome."

They were both quiet for a moment, gazes locked as the world passed them by. Dani realized she should probably say something and quickly forced her mouth to work. "That looks good. Got any recommendations for what I should try?"

Zoey's eyes slid to the side, and Dani suddenly remembered that she wasn't alone. Vernon was standing beside her, and she had the strongest urge to take a step away from him before Zoey got the wrong idea. Then again, it *was* exactly what it looked like. Dani *was* on a date with Vernon, so why did she feel the need to hide him away? She hadn't felt this way at all in the restaurant, so why the hell was she feeling differently just because Zoey was here?

"Who's your friend?" Dani turned to look at Vernon, his expression filled with curiosity as he looked back and forth between Dani and Zoey.

"This is my...friend, Vernon," Dani said finally. It wasn't exactly the truth, considering she had just met Vernon today and technically they were on a date, but anything else seemed strange. Vernon gave Dani a look before smiling and holding his hand out to Zoey.

"Right. I'm Vernon. It's very nice to meet you."

Zoey quickly switched hands, shifting the ice cream before shaking Vernon's hand and nodding. "I'm Zoey. I'm one of the librarians here in town. I don't think I've seen you before."

"Probably not. I don't live in Peach Blossom. I'm from the next town over but I have a few friends from here."

Zoey nodded, but Dani didn't know what to say. The whole situation had Dani swallowing hard with the need to say something to break the strange silence they had fallen into. Before she could come up with the right words to say, Zoey raised the ice cream in her hand before gesturing at the street.

"I should probably head out. I have a few more pages to get read before book club this week." She glanced over at Dani from beneath dark lashes. "Will I see you there again this week?"

Dani smiled widely. Book club was hands down one of the few things she now looked forward to. "Of course. I wouldn't miss it for the world." Zoey smiled, and Dani's breath hitched. It was amazing how much a smile could make you feel. For a moment, she wondered what that smile would've looked like by candlelight at the restaurant she had just left. What would Zoey have thought of the food? These were questions that Dani now wanted answers to, though she hadn't been thinking them before. What the hell was she supposed to do with that information? Dani stayed quiet, waving when Zoey glanced over her shoulder. When she turned the corner, disappearing from sight, Dani's smile fell.

Vernon coughed, reminding Dani that he was still there. "So, that explains a lot about tonight."

Dani frowned. "What do you mean?"

Vernon looked at her for a moment before continuing. "It was nice getting to know you, but I'm pretty sure that there won't be a second date. That's not a bad thing, just an observation," he added before Dani could say something in response. "I just want you to think about something for a moment, and this is not me trying to pry into your business."

Dani crossed her arms but nodded for him to continue.

"You seemed a lot more excited to see Zoey just now than you have been on our entire date."

"Well, first dates are always a little awkward, aren't they?"

He nodded. "They can be. Are you and Zoey good friends?"

"No." Dani thought for a moment, not liking the way that one-word sentence sounded. "At least not right now. I am hoping we will be eventually." Dani couldn't help but smile at the thought of getting closer to Zoey in the weeks and months to come.

"You have a really pretty smile, especially when you're thinking about things that you like," Vernon said softly. When Dani looked up, his own smile looked defeated. "And I'm pretty sure I know who you were thinking about just now. Why don't we grab some ice cream, and chat just as friends. No pressure."

Dani wasn't sure how to feel, but the more she thought on his words the more she felt something shift inside her mind. There was a possibility growing that she had never truly considered before.

Nine

Being surrounded by books and people enjoying them was usually Zoey's happy place. But today, she just couldn't seem to find her groove. She knew why, but she was doing her damnedest to fight against it. She and Dani weren't even dating—never even would be close to it given their run-in the day before, so why the hell was she letting it ruin her day?

"Why the long face, friend?"

Zoey jumped slightly at being caught being anything other than her normal self. She had hoped to get through her shift without being called out on her off behavior, but with how observant Tiffany could be, she wasn't sure why she even bothered. Rarely was she able to get anything past her friend, though she hadn't ever really tried. Controlling her facial expressions was not in Zoey's ministry. She had learned that at a young age and after being caught so many times with her thoughts all over her face, she rarely attempted to hide it anymore, even if it meant a conversation she wasn't ready to have.

"I saw Dani this weekend."

Tiffany rushed over, doing the exaggerated waddle that always had her in stitches. Now she barely could muster up a half-hearted chuckle and she knew that lack of response would be noted as well. Any thought of getting through the day without having to rehash her run-in with Dani was flying out the window with each step Tiffany took toward her, until Zoey knew they had crossed the threshold of no return.

"Okay," Tiffany replied, prompting her to keep talking. "You saw Dani as in just a random pass by, or you saw Dani as in no clothes, no shoes, all service?"

The laugh that was startled out of her had Zoey nearly doubled over. "How do you come up with this stuff? Maybe you should be the one writing books and not me."

Tiffany's grin was smug as she leaned against the counter. "Maybe I do. You don't have a monopoly on pen names. Now, explain to me why running into Dani over the weekend has you in here darkening the aisles with your despondent sighs instead of putting pep in your step?"

"I wasn't sighing despondently." When Tiffany gave her a look, she rolled her eyes. "I was brooding. There's a difference."

"Not when it comes to you. You aren't the brooding type."

Zoey wanted to push back, but she knew Tiffany was

right. Brooding wasn't something that she normally took part in. She wasn't some tall, dark and handsome bad boy with a terrible backstory in a romance novel. True, she had what some people would count as a tragic backstory, given her lack of living parents and being raised by her older brother on various army bases, but that was where the similarities ended. Sure, she could occasionally get introspective, but overall, happiness was her default state. Plus, therapy was still her best friend.

"Does this have anything to do with the fact that Dani was seen with some guy at Mama Rita's Kitchen a couple days ago?" When Zoey raised her eyebrows in surprise, Tiffany shrugged. "The devil moves fast but the gossip in this town moves faster. Overheard Mrs. P talking about it when I stopped by the grocer this morning. So, is that why you're in such a shit mood?"

"What? I don't kn—"

"Are you really going to try to lie to me right now? Seriously?" Tiffany cut in.

Zoey sighed before replying. "If you knew already then why were you trying to make me say it?"

Tiffany folded her arms and narrowed her eyes at Zoey. "Because it's called *communicating* and not *making assumptions*. Plus, now that you've actually admitted that's what is making you act like someone dog-eared a page in your favorite book, we can figure out a way to change things."

Zoey shuddered at the idea of someone harming a book like that before shaking her head and giving Tiffany a fond look. Of course, Tiffany was already trying to figure out how to fix things. It was one reason why she and Zoey got along so well. "I don't know about that, Tiff," Zoey said. "You can't fix something that's not broken. Dani and I aren't together, so there's nothing to fix. Maybe I was just giving myself false hope, reading into something that wasn't there. It wouldn't be the first time."

Zoey didn't often talk about her last relationship, but given how this was shaping up, she was starting to sense a pattern. Falling for someone who was incapable of liking you back was a trope as old as time, and apparently a recurring one in Zoey's life.

"I don't know about that, Zoey," Tiffany said, placing a hand on her shoulder. "I don't know Dani that well but from what I've heard about her, she doesn't seem like the type to lead someone on. Plus, that shit with Holly doesn't even count. Hell, I refuse to even call that a relationship because of what went down."

Tiffany wasn't wrong. It had taken Zoey a few months and a couple rounds of therapy before she realized that what she and Holly had wasn't exactly a relationship, healthy or otherwise. What had started as a friendship had morphed into some unspoken, unacknowledged thing that never should have happened when Zoey really paused to think about it. A drunken kiss between two lonely people that should have been laughed off the next day. Instead, the two of them fell into a sort of limbo that was more one-sided sexual relief than anything. The whole debacle culminated in Zoey hoping for something that had never been there, and Holly using that to her advantage before ultimately dropping Zoey like a bad habit and getting back together with her ex. Never had falling for a straight girl ever caused so much damage.

"And besides, you don't even know if Dani is straight. Maybe she was just hanging out with that guy as friends. Remember how we always talk about don't assume someone's sexuality until you get confirmation?"

Zoey rolled her eyes but nodded. "Yes, yes I know. Comphet is the thing."

"That, and Dani has not one but two lesbian sisters," Tiffany continued. "I doubt she would pull a move that would have them chewing her ass out. She doesn't seem the type."

She couldn't deny that. Dani had never even appeared to realize Zoey had an interest in her. She had been open and friendly like everyone else had been upon moving to town. She doubted Dani would pull a one-eighty and switch up on her in that way. "Other than occasionally having a conversation about books or the esports club, Dani hasn't shown any interest in me."

"Yet. She hasn't shown any interest in you yet," Tiffany added.

"Well, regardless of whether it's 'yet' or 'ever,' I can't keep going around in circles in my mind about her. I have research to finish and a deadline to hit." When a patron started walking toward their desk, Zoey figured it was the perfect time to change the subject. "Besides, it's my lunch break and I'm starving. I didn't really eat much for breakfast, so I think I'm going to head to Thomas's diner and treat myself."

Tiffany cocked an eyebrow but nodded. "I think that's an excellent idea. Mind bringing me back something? I think I'm probably going to end up working through my lunch. There's a grant that I need to finish the application for so I can send it out next week, and I am struggling."

Zoey walked around the desk, smiling and waving at the patron before she replied, "Of course. Want me to bring back your usual?"

"You know it. And say hi to Thomas for me if you see him," Tiffany said before turning to greet the man who just walked in. Zoey nodded before making her way to the doors.

Despite her down mood, she couldn't help but smile when she exited the library. It was a perfect spring day with a gentle breeze that carried only a hint of crispness. The sun was out, rays beaming down and warming her skin. It was impossible to stay in a crap mood when the day was as perfect as it was. The walk to Thomas's diner helped Zoey clear her head, and she really thought about Tiffany's words. Perhaps Zoey's past was clouding her judgment when it came to Dani. It wasn't fair to compare Dani to her ex. She knew that. But it was still difficult when she wasn't the most outgoing to begin with. Flirting and expressing interest had always been difficult for her. She knew she needed to be more assertive when it came to these types of things, but Zoey didn't even know the first step to take on how to change her ways. Maybe she should have grabbed a book on dating to read over lunch.

When she stepped into Thomas's diner, the familiar greeting from the servers helped push her concerns from her mind. It was lunchtime so the diner was crowded. Although they normally only got thirty minutes for lunch, because things were a bit slow that day, she knew that Tiffany would be okay with Zoey taking a little bit longer, especially if she came back with lunch for her.

Zoey waved when Thomas was the one who walked over to her. "Hey, Zoey. Just you today?"

"Yep, it's just me, though I do plan on bringing Tiffany back some lunch. If it's too crowded, I can always get mine to go."

Thomas rubbed the back of his neck before turning to look around the dining room. "It is a little crowded, but maybe we could fit you in if you don't mind sharing a table with someone."

"I don't mind sharing."

Zoey froze when she heard that familiar voice. She turned just in time to see Dani walk over.

Dani continued. "It's just me today so you're more than welcome to share a table."

Zoey felt her heartbeat kick into overdrive, and she tried not to let her fight-or-flight reaction kick in. Sometimes, she wondered if the universe was just playing a massive practical joke on her and sitting back to see how she reacted. Then again, she figured maybe it was just the nature of small towns. Nine times out of ten, if you were thinking about someone, the next time you went into town, chances are you'd see them. Zoey realized that she hadn't said anything, and she quickly moved to respond. "I'd love to share a table with you, if you really don't mind. I don't want to disturb you during your lunchtime if you need a break from people."

Dani smiled and Zoey felt the need to scream. It should be illegal for someone to have a smile so nice. "A break from people, sure. But I don't need a break from you."

Damn. Zoey wasn't sure how to take that without giving herself false hope. If those words had come from someone else, she would have thought they were flirting with her. But from Dani, she wasn't sure if she was reading too much into it because that was just what she was hoping for. Zoey glanced over at Thomas. His expression hadn't changed, but she could swear he was laughing at her.

"Um, if you're sure."

Dani nodded. "Of course I am. Come on. I have the booth over here."

Zoey followed, nodding hello to the few patrons she recognized. She was trying to look everywhere except at Dani and how good she looked in her baby blue scrubs. When her gaze just happened to slide over giving her a glimpse of the way the fabric molded to the shape of Dani's ass, she couldn't help but stare. *I'm no better than a man*, she thought, quickly averting her gaze when Dani stopped.

"Feel free to choose whichever side."

Zoey nodded before sliding into the booth. She pretended she wasn't watching when Dani slid in across from her and picked up the menu. Zoey knew exactly what she wanted when it came to food. She knew what she wanted when it came to the woman across from her too.

"Thanks for letting me sit with you," Zoey said, trying not to look as awkward as she felt. Dani glanced at her from over the menu.

"Of course," she replied simply before looking back at the menu. Zoey looked down at the table as they waited for the waitress and fought against the need to drum her fingers. The familiar diner sounds created a backdrop that kept the silence from being grating. Still, there was a strange tension between them, and Zoey wasn't sure how to break it. She wasn't surprised when it was Dani who spoke up first.

"So, how has your workday been?"

Zoey sighed softly in relief. Work was an easy enough topic to talk about. "Everyone's back in school so it tends to be very quiet during the day. It's easier to get things done before the afternoon when more people start coming in."

Dani nodded. "I can see that. I've come in during the day a couple times when I didn't feel like actually eating on my lunch break, and it's always nice to be able to wander through the stacks and just kind of exist for a minute."

That she could relate to. Her brother had often asked her if working at the library was boring when she was just putting books back in their respective places, but

Zoey had always found it the perfect time to be alone. The repetitive motion of walking around and putting the books on their shelves always helped her clear her mind, and she enjoyed those times just as much as she enjoyed talking with the other patrons and helping them figure out what books and resources they were looking for. Working at the library also gave her time to do a little research for her books or jot down some thoughts when her muse decided to give her an idea for a scene. Some of her best ideas came when she was walking through the aisles, returning books to their proper places. It was like the pages whispered to her, sprinkling a bit of their wisdom. She loved it.

"On that, we are in complete agreement," Zoey replied, looking up at Dani with a hesitant smile. Dani grinned and it loosened something in her chest. Perhaps they could be friends. It wouldn't be such a bad thing, even with Zoey's feelings. She would get over it eventually and besides, there was nothing wrong with having more friends. Maybe it was for the best anyway. She didn't even know if she would be in Peach Blossom long term. Everything was dependent on the budget, and she still didn't know if there would be money in the budget for her to stay after her contract ended. And even if they did decide to offer her a permanent position, did she even want to stay? Doing research about a small town for her book setting was one thing, but after the book was written and done, would she want to stay?

When their waitress came, Zoey and Dani gave their

orders before settling in and exchanging anecdotes about their workdays. The conversation flowed easily and more of Zoey's nervousness melted away in the face of Dani's obvious interest in their conversation. Zoey tried to keep her thoughts firmly on friendship, even as her mind cataloged everything from the way Dani's lips wrapped around her straw to the way she licked her fingers after each chip. At one point, she dropped her pickle when she glanced up and witnessed Dani, finger in her mouth and her eyes closed as she sucked off the salt. Zoey quickly recovered, grabbing her pickle and taking a hard bite, hoping that the motion and noise would get her mind off other things.

"Didn't you say you needed to order something else?" Dani asked as she pushed her now-empty plate away. Zoey frowned before she remembered Tiffany's request.

"Oh, yes. Thank you for reminding me." She quickly called out to their waitress to put the order in. She didn't need to get back from lunch and immediately be met with an angrily hungry Tiffany. She was not a nice person when she was hungry, especially if her not having food was someone else's fault.

"So, are you bringing the food back for someone special?" Dani asked. The question was phrased nonchalantly, and Zoey took it at face value.

"No, just bringing back lunch for my coworker, Tiffany, since she was planning on working through hers." Zoey smiled down at the table as she started ripping apart her napkin, just to have something else to do. "I felt kind of bad because I was a little down in the dumps this morning and she was trying to cheer me up."

"Oh, I'm sorry. Is there anything I can do?"

Zoey shook her head. "Inviting me to sit with you for lunch was enough. Thank you though."

"Are you sure?" Dani asked. "We could go get some ice cream. It always puts me in a better mood." Her expression was so earnest that it brought a smile to Zoey's face. That was, until she remembered last night.

"Speaking of ice cream, how was last night? Your... date?" Zoey internally cringed at how curious she sounded. She had hoped to thread the question in more smoothly, but this was the only opening she could think of that would seem natural enough and not just coming out of nowhere.

Dani shrugged, her fingers playing with the rim of her glass. Zoey couldn't help but lock onto that tiny motion, staring at the way Dani's fingers slowly circled. The question had been on her mind since she sat down, and Dani had given her the perfect opening to ask. Maybe she was a masochist for wanting to know how well Dani's date went with another person. Still, the question was already out there, and it would be even stranger to take it back. She was going to have to see it through.

"Vernon was a nice guy, but the date itself wasn't really anything exciting."

It took everything in her to not smile. Zoey knew it was a dick move to be happy that Dani's date didn't turn out well, but she would deal with the karmic retribution later. "Oh? I'm sorry to hear that. Are you guys going to try to go out again?" Zoey asked, trying not to sound too interested in Dani's response.

Dani shook her head. "Probably not. He wasn't feeling it either, though I don't know if that was because of my own lack of interest in him or not. Either way, it's probably for the best."

"Why?"

Dani paused for a moment before dropping her chin down in her hand. She hummed softly, drawing her in. Her gaze was down, and it looked faraway like she was seeing some scenario that was invisible to the rest of the world. Zoey waited patiently. She wanted to hear more, and she doubted that pushing was going to be the way to go.

Finally, Dani looked up. "I'm trying to work some things out for myself, and dating Vernon would not have been conducive to that."

"Oh," Zoey breathed out as she tried to figure out what that could potentially mean.

"Yeah," Dani responded. "You know how sometimes your entire perspective can shift just based off one event?"

"Sure." It wasn't a lie just to keep her talking. Zoey truly understood. She'd had a few moments like that herself and understood that sometimes all it took was something small to start a wave of change in your life.

"Let's just say that I am having a change of perspective," Dani said. The conversation was interrupted by the waitress bringing the check and the to-go box with Tiffany's food.

Zoey wanted to send her away. The conversation with Dani was just getting going and she wanted more. She was gluttonous for more information. She wanted to hear everything and spend hours probing Dani's mind. Still, she knew it would be rude to leave Tiffany waiting too long to eat. With an internal sigh, she reached for the check, but before she touched it, Dani snatched it up with a grin. "I got this."

"You don't have to," Zoey countered.

"Consider it a thank-you from a loyal library patron. Jordan talks so much about how he loves the esports league and it's nice to see him so interested in something these days."

Zoey nodded and dropped her hand. She watched Dani pull out her card and thought quickly. She had to go back to work, but she wanted to spend more time with Dani. It wouldn't be weird to ask her out again, would it? They could be casual about things. Friendly even. She had to take advantage of this moment, otherwise Zoey knew she would regret not giving it a try.

"If you're not doing anything later tonight, there's a movie I was planning to see if you'd like to go with me?" She internally patted herself on the back for getting the invitation out without stuttering over her words. She had done her best to phrase the invitation casually as to not arouse suspicion, but she couldn't help the way her heart pounded as she waited for Dani's response.

Dani looked up from under long lashes. She signed the receipt before speaking. "Unfortunately, I can't. I have Jordan this week and everyone else has plans tonight."

"Oh," Zoey said, trying not to sound as disappointed as she felt. "That's okay."

"But," Dani continued, "I'm free tomorrow night if that works for you?"

"Yeah. That works totally fine," Zoey replied with a wide grin. She knew she probably looked ridiculous for being so excited about a simple yes to getting together again. Friends did this all the time, so it shouldn't have been as big of a deal as it was to her.

"Great. It's a date then."

Zoey was shocked into silence as Dani stood up and slid out of the booth. "Have a great rest of your day."

"Right. You too." Zoey watched as Dani walked to the door and waved when she glanced back. When Dani finally disappeared from view, Zoey was still in disbelief of what just happened.

Date?

Ten

Dani Williams was not the type of person who freaked out at small things. She was cool. Calm. Collected even. So, coming up with the words to explain how she was feeling right now was almost an insurmountable task.

Having lunch with Zoey had made her acutely aware of just how attractive she found the other woman. It wasn't like Dani had never found other women cute. Hell, she had eyes and was secure enough in herself to recognize that certain attributes were attractive, no matter who had them. She knew the other woman was cute; had even told her that once or twice before. But this realization of just how attractive she was and that it wasn't just in a platonic way was new. Or was it? Dani was quickly realizing that she was far more observant about other people than she was when it came to herself. That was probably something she should work on.

"Oh hell," she said to herself as she sank down on her

bed. The rest of the workday had been uneventful. She had gone back to work, her mind still replaying their lunch and how easy it had been compared to every single date she had gone on recently. When Zoey had invited her to a movie, Dani had immediately wanted to say yes. She couldn't help but marvel at how excited she had been at the thought of spending more time with her, even if they were simply sitting in the dark and staring at a screen. Her excitement had been momentarily dashed when she realized that she would have to decline.

Being a single parent was difficult in that way. Jordan was home tonight, and she knew everyone else had plans already. Dani had quickly offered the following night and when Zoey readily agreed that excitement was renewed. Being this excited to hang out with someone who wasn't already a friend or family was novel to her. Every invitation previously, Dani *had* said yes, but with the type of reluctance that often left her wondering if she should've just said no. This wasn't even a real date, despite what she'd thrown out before fleeing the scene. And yet she still found herself anticipating the time they would eventually be spending together.

When Dani had gotten back to work, Natasha had been curious about her shift in mood. Before leaving for lunch, Dani had given her the rundown of the date with Vernon. She had made sure to emphasize how nice of a guy he was, even while insisting that Dani didn't see any sort of romantic future with him. She had expected Natasha to throw out another name or insist that maybe she should give it a second date and see if maybe nerves had just kept Dani from really getting into things, but that wasn't what happened. No, Natasha had started asking the type of questions that had been on Dani's mind for weeks. It was like holding up a mirror where everywhere you turned, it was there.

When Dani had thrown out the "date" comment, she had seen Zoey's eyes widen before Dani had turned tail and made her escape. Here she was, nearly thirty years old and running away from her own words. It was like she wasn't even an adult. But now as she took the time to really think back on her conversation with Zoey, she realized one undeniable truth. She liked Zoey and she was pretty sure it wasn't just in the friendly-neighborhood-librarian type of way. Even though she knew that this would bring her nothing but grief, Dani decided she needed to consult with her sisters.

With a sigh, she stood and walked across the hall. She knocked on Ava's door, giving herself time to calm down before opening it when Ava called out. She wasn't surprised to see Ava sitting at her desk, her fingers flying furiously over her laptop. Ava paused to turn to look over at Dani. "You actually knocked and waited for me to tell you to come in." Her eyes narrowed as she looked at Dani. "What did you do?"

Dani rolled her eyes. "I didn't do a damn thing. I just... there's something I wanted to talk to you about if you have a minute."

Ava watched her for a moment before turning around

in her chair. "There's something you want to talk to me about? Is everything all right?"

Dani shook her head and then nodded. That granted her an eyebrow arch from Ava and a considering look.

"Well, that was clear as mud," Ava replied.

"That's about how I feel about all this, so that tracks," Dani said, walking into the room. She sat on Ava's bed and tried not to look like she was having a quarter-life crisis. With her eyes trained on the floor, Dani tried to figure out how to start this conversation. Did she immediately dive into her not-quite date with Zoey? Should she bring up how she felt on all the disastrous dates she'd had over the past few months, if not years?

"You're starting to worry me," Ava said, bringing Dani's attention back to the fact that she was now sitting in front of a live audience. "What's going on?"

Deciding that the best course of action was just to dive in and not think too much about it, Dani took a few deep breaths before speaking. "How did you know that you were gay?"

The silence between them stretched as if all the air was sucked from the room. Ava's dumbstruck expression had Dani wishing for a camera. If not for how serious she felt the conversation was, Dani would've laughed at Ava's wide eyes and her mouth that seemed to be frozen open. She didn't get why Ava was having such an extreme reaction to her question. It's not that they had never talked about sexuality before. Well, they had talked about Ava and later Vini's sexualities. Dani had never had this conversation about herself. It was always just understood that she dated men. Hell, she had been married. She had a kid. But she was quickly realizing that those facts didn't mean shit. Especially not when she closed her eyes at night and dark brown eyes, kissable lips and curls that made her want to bury her fingers in them were the stars of her fantasies.

"What is this conversation? Are you coming out? Is this...were you in the closet?" Ava asked, her voice growing higher with each question.

Dani wanted to shrug to disperse the seriousness of the conversation and the tension that filled the air, but she knew that would only send Ava into more of a spiral. Based on Ava's mouth opening and closing with no other words being said, Dani could only conclude that she had somehow broken her sister.

"Are you okay?"

"Am I okay?" Ava asked, sounding borderline hysterical. "You just asked me if I was gay."

"No, I asked you how you knew you were gay," Dani corrected. "There's a difference. Besides, I know you're Grace-sexual. You hate everyone else."

"That's not..." Ava trailed off when Dani gave her a look. "Fine. But don't try to change the subject. This is about you. Where is this all coming from?"

Dani shrugged and crossed her arms. She didn't want to seem too serious, even though she could almost feel her heart rate increasing. "Nowhere really. We just haven't really talked about this stuff in a while."

"Nowhere, huh?" Ava gave her a considering look. "Does this sudden questioning of my sexuality have anything to do with Jordan's new favorite librarian?"

Dani looked down, picking at a small fuzzy thread on Ava's comforter. "I don't know what you're talking about." Ava crossed her arms and gave Dani a withering look. "Ugh, fine. Tell me what you know."

Ava turned around fully in her chair. "I know that when Grace and I ran into the cutie in cardigans at Terry's, she was awfully curious about you."

"What was she curious about?" Dani asked before she could stop herself. "Did she say anything about me?" She knew she was being obvious in her quest for more information about Zoey, but the ship to being coy had clearly sailed.

"Just that she had given you some advice and was worried that perhaps you had taken her words the wrong way." Dani frowned but Ava continued before she could say anything. "I told her that if you had taken it the wrong way, you would've let her know immediately. Everyone knows you aren't that polite."

Dani shrugged. "You're not wrong. She did give me some advice that was very helpful." Dani narrowed her eyes. "Was that all she said about me?"

"Why does it matter?" Ava asked. "Did you want her to say something else about you?"

Dani thought about it. She could've said no, but that would've been a lie. She knew if she wanted Ava's advice, she had to lay it all out there. Ava was stubborn as hell when she wanted to be, so the fact that Dani was getting this much was a damn miracle, and one she needed to continue.

"Yes."

"Like?" Ava prompted.

Dani sighed and looked up at the ceiling as she leaned back on her hands. "Like if she thought I was nice to look at."

"Vanity? Really, Dani?"

Dani clenched her jaw before continuing. "I think she's cute and I think I fucking like her, so yes. Vanity." Ava's answering silence had Dani lifting her head to look at her. Even with Ava acting like she knew it all, her expression was shocked. Dani would have laughed if not for the subject of their conversation.

"Holy shit," Ava whispered. "You're gay?"

"No." Dani paused and thought. "Yes? I don't know. I just know that when Zoey asked me to a movie, I was more excited than I have been in a long fucking time."

"Yeah, but friends go to movies together all the time."

Dani arched an eyebrow. "Do friends go to the movies with the desire to make out? Do friends fantasize about each other?"

"Wow," Ava replied, looking at Dani as if she was seeing her for the first time. "How the hell have you never stopped to think that you liked women too? You were the one Vini and I talked to when we came out."

The question was valid and yet Dani didn't have an answer. "I don't know," she replied, frustration bubbling within her like a pot of boiling water left unattended on the stove. "I just never really had time to think about it. Mom was sick and then there was school. After school, there was Jordan and Mom's funeral. Vini was so young, and Dad was almost unable to cope, and you were so angry, Ava."

Dani stood up, the energy she felt sending her pacing around the room as she thought back over all of the years that she might have lost not being able to look inward. She had clearly missed such a massive part of herself, and it was damn near overwhelming.

"And I get it, Ava. I understood why you were angry because you had to give up a lot of things to come back, but it just meant that I did my best to try to keep things as smooth as possible. I wanted to make sure home was one of the last things you had to worry about on top of everything else, and that meant putting everything else on the back burner." Dani's voice faded away as she thought about the years spent on everything other than figuring out her own shit. She wasn't upset with her family. They were all just doing what they needed to do to get through loss and grief. She was just frustrated that there could've been something so big inside herself that she never got a chance to uncover or understand—until now, when it seemed like it was almost too late.

"Wow."

Dani stopped when she heard Vini's voice and turned. Ava was still seated at her desk, but now her hand was holding up the phone with Vini's face on the screen. Dani hadn't realized Ava had called her in, but she appreciated not having to have this conversation twice.

"I'm sorry, Dani." Vini's voice was uncharacteristically subdued, and that plus Ava's expression cooled some of Dani's frustration. "I don't think I ever really thought about everything you were juggling back then."

"It's okay," Dani said, trying to halt any apologies. She wasn't bringing these things up to make her sisters feel bad, but it felt cathartic to get it out. "We were all doing what we needed to do. I'm not upset about any of it."

Ava spoke up. "I know, but still. I'm sorry too, sis."

While she appreciated the apologies, it wasn't what Dani wanted to hear right now. Right now, she wanted to make sense of the thoughts and feelings inside her, but how could she do all that when she didn't have a playbook? She didn't have a plan for how it should all go. She wasn't even sure if this was something that Ava or Vini could understand. Thinking back to the conversations they'd all had back when they were younger and hormones had made their appearances, both Ava and Vini had known right away who they were and the gender they liked. But here Dani was, having these thoughts years later when she should conceivably already know who she was.

She felt like she was starting from scratch. In a way, she felt almost juvenile, and it led to more frustration. Frustration at having to figure all this out at the eleventh hour like she was standing on a cliff, teetering at the edge and not sure if she had a parachute on or not. Dani had a life and a career and a kid for crying out loud. How was it she was just now figuring out whether she liked women or not. It shouldn't have been a big deal, but where did she go from here? How did she talk to Jordan about this? *Did* she talk to Jordan about this? She had barely talked to him about going on dates with men. He knew that occasionally she went out because he would stay home with either his aunts or his grandad, but Dani had always said she wouldn't introduce Jordan to anyone she dated until after at least six months, and only if the relationship was headed to something more long-lasting and serious. But he had already met Zoey; saw her more than Dani did in fact. What happened if something went terribly wrong and that messed up the relationship between him and his favorite librarian?

"It's fine," Dani says finally. She walked back over and sank back down onto the bed like her strings had been cut. "It's all fine. I just…don't know what to do now. I'm going out with Zoey tomorrow, and I don't know if I should say something about this or not."

"You do whatever you feel like you need to," Vini said. "There's no timetable for life, Dani. You can just feel things out and take your time."

"And Zoey seems like a really good person," Ava added in. "I think if you talk to her about things that she'll understand."

"You think?" Dani asked, uncharacteristically vulnerable in a way that felt simultaneously good and terrifying. She wanted to force her voice to be stronger, firmer, more like her usual self. But if she couldn't be vulnerable with her sisters, then who else could she be this way with? Zoey's face flashed in her mind and she was surprised but also intrigued that maybe this could be a new beginning.

"I mean," Ava said, pulling her attention again. "I always sensed at the very least some bisexual energy from Zoey. No straight woman would have those many cardigans and I'm pretty sure she drives a Subaru."

"Those are really reliable cars," Vini jumped in. "Much better than Ava's shitty Prius."

"My Prius is a very economical car!"

Dani laughed softly as Ava and Vini bickered over the line. It gave her some time to come to terms with such a big shift in her mind. Dani still had so many questions for herself, and only the knowledge that she had people she could go to kept the panic at bay. If she had realized this about herself earlier, would she have been in a different relationship? Would she have found the love of her life sooner? Would she have even stayed in Peach Blossom? How differently would her life have gone had she even considered the possibility?

Eleven

Was it possible to feel like a kid with a new crush when you were almost thirty and just meeting a potential new friend for a movie? If it was, that would describe how Dani felt as she walked up to the movie theater. She had spent part of last night coming up with strategies with Vini and Ava for how she could subtly get an idea if Zoey was interested in women or not. Most of them had been overly complicated and borderline ridiculous, but Dani couldn't help but admit that it felt good to joke around with her sisters again in a way they hadn't done in a while. Their lives were quickly changing lanes, but she was feeling a bit better about things, thanks to their conversation.

Now though, she had to figure out the best way to incorporate some of it in. She had gone with Ava's suggestion of dressing up a bit more than she would have if she was just meeting Natasha for a movie. Dani had gone with a pair of tight jeans and a loose blouse that she left partially unbuttoned. She had scoured various Pinterest boards, trying to find the perfect outfit for her first queer not-quite-date. Most of the ideas had left her frustrated and more than a little confused. She was definitely not hip to the lingo when it came to the queer scene. She still didn't even know what to label herself. How was she supposed to figure out where she fit in when she wasn't even sure if this was a date at all? If Zoey wasn't interested in dating women, how else would Dani figure all this out? She pushed those thoughts away to save for a different time. For now, she needed to concentrate on tonight and take it from there.

The sun was just starting to set, and Dani could feel the air starting to cool when she made it to the theater. Her gaze fell on Zoey standing in front of the doors, and Dani didn't bother trying to stop her smile. Now that she was aware of it, she could recognize how everything in her perked up at the sight of Zoey. She had her hair pulled back in a chunky braid tonight, leaving her neck bare, and Dani wondered if she brushed her fingers over Zoey's skin if it would be as soft as it looked. She had forgone her usual cardigan, and instead was wearing a tight black shirt tucked into a pair of wide-legged jeans. It was almost jarring to see her dressed so differently, and belatedly, Dani wondered if Zoey had changed up her style for her.

When Zoey caught sight of Dani, her wide grin had Dani feeling energized and she had to fight to keep herself from bounding up to her like a lovestruck puppy. Zoey's normal glasses were gone today, giving Dani unfettered access to her dark brown gaze—a gaze that seemed to turn several degrees hotter when they landed on Dani. Zoey's eyes dropped before slowly making their way back up Dani's body. With anyone else, Dani would have immediately known it was *on* with that look alone. She could almost feel it like a physical caress on her skin, and she looked over her with the same intensity.

"Zoey," Dani said, not sure what to say next. What were the rules of going on a not-quite-date with another woman? Should they hug? Would that be weird, considering Dani never gave more than a handshake to the men she had gone out with? "Glad to see you. You look amazing."

Dani couldn't help the slight breathlessness of her voice, but when Zoey smiled widely, she wanted to ply her with even more compliments. It might have been evening, but her smile was enough to light up the night sky.

"You look really good too," Zoey said as she gave Dani another once-over. She held up her hand. "I hope you don't mind, but I already bought the tickets."

Holy hell. Maybe it really is a date. On the outside, she appeared calm, but on the inside, she was a mess of emotions. There was nervousness and anticipation for what the night might bring. Ava was staying at the house with Jordan, so Dani wasn't expected to be home early. She wasn't sure what Zoey might have in mind for after the movie. Dani had a few ideas just in case, and Ava had made a few suggestions, though Dani wasn't sure if she was ready for some of the more intense ones on Ava's list. This was the first time she and Zoey would be alone together. She didn't want to come on too strong and scare her away, or get too over her head that she was the one who turned tail and ran.

They walked side by side into the movie theater. A couple of people were milling about in the lobby and when Dani and Zoey walked around them, the backs of their hands brushed together. It was such an innocuous touch and yet a zing of electricity shot up Dani's arm. It made her want to reach out and tangle her fingers with Zoey's, but until she knew that this was truly a date, she didn't feel comfortable taking that next step. Hand-holding wasn't something you could justify unless someone was about to fall in a hole or something else equally perilous. If this were a first date with her and a guy, she similarly wouldn't feel comfortable taking their hand, so Dani gave herself a bit of grace. They walked over to the snack counter and when it was their turn to order, she turned to Zoey.

"Since you bought the movie tickets, the snacks are on me. Unless you like Goobers in which case you'll have to pay for that shit yourself because those things are disgusting."

Zoey laughed, her nose wrinkling in the cutest way that had Dani staring. How she hadn't realized that her thoughts of Zoey's cuteness weren't just innocent observations she would never know. Now that she recognized it for what it was, she couldn't stop cataloging all of the cute things about Zoey. How her nose crinkled when she smiled. How the brown of her eyes looked so incredibly warm and inviting, whether they were behind lenses or not. It wasn't just platonic admiration. No, she was attractive in a way that made Dani want to touch.

"On that we are in complete agreement," Zoey replied. She turned to look over the menu. "I was thinking about going for the kettle corn popcorn and maybe some Skittles. What were you thinking?"

I was thinking about how cute you are was what Dani wanted to say. *I was thinking that I want to kiss you* was a close second. Instead, she replied, "Kettle corn popcorn sounds great to me. The Skittles are all yours but I'm thinking about the Reese's Pieces. Kind of like Skittles' distant cousin." Dani was rewarded by another of Zoey's sweet laughs. She felt amazingly proud that the night had just began and already she was keeping her entertained.

"They are kind of like cousins, aren't they? I never really thought about that before, but it makes a lot of sense," Zoey said. Once they finished ordering, Dani was happy enough to pass over her card and pay for everything. She was finding herself enjoying this even give-and-take. There had always been a sort of pressure during her previous dates, whereas with Zoey, they seemed to fall into things easily. Dani wasn't sure if it was because they were both women, or if it was because they both were who they were. Either way, she was finding herself smiling as they grabbed their food and moved to find their theater.

After finding their seats they settled in, talking softly

before the previews began. Luckily enough, the theater had gone through a renovation a couple of years ago, replacing the previous seats with lounging chairs that allowed for easy sharing. They both, under an unspoken agreement, pushed their chairs back and moved the armrest between them to set the popcorn in place so they both could easily reach. It reminded Dani of lounging on the recliner at home, but this time with a cutie by her side, and damn, wasn't that a kick in the pants.

Even with this being the only movie theater within a thirty-minute drive, it never really got crowded, which Dani could appreciate. Then again, she didn't often go to the movies on opening nights so she couldn't speak to those experiences. Jordan wasn't really into most movies, so she had only had to suffer through crowded theaters once or twice so far. Now, by the time the previews began there were only a few other couples and groups in the theater, but they were spread out enough that she and Zoey had the whole row to themselves. Dani sent up thanks to whichever deity was listening. She was thankful there wouldn't be anyone else close enough to notice her anxiety as she tried to figure out which of Ava's and Vini's strategies she would utilize to see if Zoey was interested in more than just a friendly night at the movie theater. Ironically enough, it was the popcorn that gave her the perfect chance to test the waters.

As they settled into the movie, they took turns taking handfuls of popcorn from the tub between the two of them. Dani would glance down every now and then to see Zoey's fingers drop down, collect a few kernels and then reach back up, popping them in her mouth. Once or twice, she was distracted looking at Zoey's lips, but she always ripped her eyes away before she got caught staring. Dani had just gotten lost in the opening scenes when she realized that her timing was off. She reached into the tub of popcorn but instead of grabbing kernels she felt the soft touch of Zoey's fingers. She paused, as did Zoey.

She had a couple options here. She could move away, grab the popcorn, and keep eating like nothing had happened and it was a simple slipup. Or, she could acknowledge it and go a step further. She knew what she wanted to do, but as time passed, she started to lose her nerve. Zoey hadn't moved away either, but when her fingers didn't move into the hold, Dani sighed softly and shifted, grabbing a few kernels of popcorn. The moment seemed to break and a loud noise from the screen made both of them jump.

So much for that, Dani thought as she mentally berated herself for chickening out. For the rest of the movie, their fingers would occasionally brush, but Dani didn't think about making a move. She needed to come up with a new strategy, but the movie soon caught her interest, and she found herself engrossed in the plot as it played out on the screen. By the time the movie ended, Dani was nearly in tears and when she glanced over at Zoey, she was relieved to see her in the same state. They both moved to leave the theater, dropping their empty snack boxes in the trash before walking out and into a darkened night.

"That was amazing," Zoey said, her lips split in a wide smile. She brushed a finger under her eyes. "A little sad and definitely very emotional, but still so good."

"It was," Dani agreed. "I had to hide a very womanly sniffle in the popcorn that last time. I thought you were going to burst into tears."

Zoey laughed and pushed against Dani with her shoulder. "Me? Didn't you just say you had to hide a sniffle?" Dani laughed along with her. "Do you need to get home?"

Dani shook her head. "Jordan is having an auntie night with Ava, and told me not to come home too early." At Zoey's questioning look, Dani went on to explain. "The two of them love watching scary movies and I hate it. So, when I go out, he and Ava buy a bunch of junk food, build a fort in the living room and watch all the scary movies I refuse to see."

"Ah," Zoey replied. "That sounds like a lot of fun."

Dani groaned and shook her head. "Don't tell me you like scary movies too? You seemed so normal and wholesome."

Zoey smirked and cocked her head to the side. "Don't let the cardigans and glasses fool you. I love scary movies, especially when they don't explain everything so you're left wondering what could be real."

Dani snorted, shaking her head again. "I will leave that stuff to you guys."

"So, if you don't have to get home just yet, do you

want to come over to mine and have a drink? It seems a waste to let you go home too early."

Dani swallowed hard but nodded. Anticipation and excitement warred in her mind. It wouldn't be the first time she went to Zoey's of course, but it would be the first time they were alone. "I'd love to."

It wasn't until they were both seated together on her sofa that Dani realized this was another chance to see if Zoey was interested in this as more than just friends. But now that they were really and truly alone, Dani's nerves were threatening to undo her. Zoey was perfect. She was like the sweetest combination of nice and just the right amount of sarcastic to keep Dani laughing and on her toes.

"And right when I went to put the last book on the stack, the whole thing fell down, barely missing Tiffany's head. I thought for sure she was going to clock me over the head with the thesaurus."

Dani chuckled and shook her head. "I probably would have thought about doing it too if I were her." She sat back, resting her head on the back cushions of the sofa. Zoey mirrored her as their laughter died down until they were both sitting there staring into one another's eyes. Dani wasn't sure what it was that propelled her to act, but before she realized what she planned to do, her lips were pressed to Zoey's in a soft kiss.

Shock had Dani freezing and she could feel when Zoey jerked as well. It was that startled motion that had Dani ripping her lips away and shooting up from the sofa with stuttered apologies.

"I am so sorry. I should go." Dani moved to flee, but a hand on her arm stopped her in place.

"Wait. Don't go," Zoey said.

"I should," Dani insisted. "I just kissed you when you were being nice enough to invite me out. I didn't mean to make things weird."

"You didn't," she insisted. Her hand slid down until it gripped Dani's. "I've been wanting to kiss you all night, but I was never sure if it was the right time."

Dani turned to face Zoey fully. "Really?"

She nodded. "If I'm being honest, I've been wanting to kiss you since that day in the library when you asked me for book advice." Zoey looked away, though her grip on Dani's hand didn't waver. "I wasn't sure if you were into women, but I wanted to spend some time with you. Even if it was just as friends."

Dani smiled softly as she looked down at their hands. She clasped her fingers around Zoey's and gave them a slight squeeze. "I wasn't sure if you were into women either."

"Seriously? The cardigan? The glasses? None of that screamed at least *queer* to you?"

Dani shrugged as she chuckled. "I mean, maybe? I'm so used to my sisters being explicitly out that I never really stopped to think about it."

"I drive a Subaru for fuck's sake."

Dani's laughter was soon buried beneath Zoey's lips

as they kissed again. Dani closed her eyes, enjoying the feeling of pillow-soft lips pressing against her own. She hadn't kissed Vernon, but the guy she had kissed before him hadn't even come close to feeling like this. Dani felt this kiss down to the very marrow of her bones and she brought her free hand up to cup Zoey's cheek. She marveled at the warmth in her skin and let the faint floral scent wrap around her. Everything about Zoey felt different than what Dani was used to, but instead of making her nervous, it settled her in a way she had never experienced. She sank into their kiss like a woman half-starved and when Zoey's lips parted slightly, Dani took it as the invitation it was.

She wasn't sure how long they stood in Zoey's living room trading kisses back and forth as the air heated up between them, but just when Dani was going to suggest moving things to a new location, her phone rang, startling them both. If not for the hold she now had on Zoey's shoulder, Dani might have jumped away. As it was, it took her a few moments to realize that the phone ringing was her own and it was Jordan's ringtone.

"Sorry about that," Dani said, digging her phone out of her pocket. "It's Jordan so I should..."

Zoey nodded and smiled, drawing Dani's attention down to her kiss-bruised lips. "Right. It's no problem."

Dani couldn't tear her gaze away even as she connected the call. "Hey, Jordan. What's going on?"

"Auntie Ava and I are done watching the movies. When are you coming home?"

Dani finally looked away as she reassured him, "I'll be home in just a bit. I promise." She disconnected the call and then gave Zoey an apologetic look. "I'm so sorry."

She waved her off. "There's no reason to be sorry, Dani. You're a mom. Jordan comes first." She squeezed their hands together. "Plus, we should probably take things slow. I know you said this is all new for you and I don't want to push you too quickly."

As much as Dani wanted to go quickly, she knew Zoey was right. This was new for her, and she couldn't rush into things half-cocked without thinking everything through. "I know you're right, but I do still want to get to know you."

Zoey smiled. "I want to get to know you too."

Dani took a step closer to her. "And getting to know you can include kissing right?" She couldn't help the way her gaze dropped back to Zoey's lips. She was emboldened when Zoey's gaze landed on her lips as well.

"Oh, absolutely."

Dani smiled as she leaned in again. A couple minutes delay getting home wouldn't be a bad thing, right?

Twelve

"Well, look at you smiling wide like you just won the lottery."

Zoey couldn't help but smile wider at Tiffany's words. She felt a lot like she had won the lottery. It had been a week since the movie date with Dani, and the two of them had seen each other just about every day. They had met up for lunch at Thomas's diner three times so far this week and with each meeting, Zoey felt like she couldn't get enough. Their conversations always seemed to flow so well from one subject to the next and Dani had seemed genuinely interested in what she had to say. If that wasn't enough to have Zoey sighing happily with a dopey smile on her face, then the kisses they always exchanged before separating definitely did it.

It wasn't like she had kissed tons of people, but she could confidently say that kissing Dani was like magic. Her lips were always the right mix of soft and firm as they moved against her own. For as little experience as Dani claimed to have, her kisses were enough to have Zoey wishing she hadn't said they should go slow. How the hell was it possible to get drunk off someone else's kisses? If she didn't know any better, she'd say Dani was a siren who had bewitched her.

"I won the life lottery," Zoey said, finally not bothering to take her eyes off the computer screen in front of her. They had just gotten in a shipment of new books, and she was working on getting them all logged into the system and tagged so they could be sorted and placed on their respective shelves.

Tiffany gave her a look. "I have a love-hate relationship with seeing you all smiley and happy. It's so cute it's disgusting," Tiffany said. Zoey couldn't help but laugh. She knew exactly what Tiffany was talking about because she had felt the same way about other couples that she saw around town before getting together with Dani. They hadn't yet had a conversation about the exclusivity between the two of them since they were taking things slow, but Zoey was okay with that for now. So far, this had been the healthiest relationship she had ever been in. They did just as much talking as they did kissing. And there definitely was a fair amount of that. Even if they hadn't formally decided on the label of *girlfriends*, Zoey was comfortable with how things were progressing.

"I'm going to take that as a compliment," Zoey said with a wide smile. She looked up at Tiffany and had to cover her mouth to keep from laughing out loud at her disgruntled expression. "Weren't you the one telling me to take a chance to begin with? How are you going to act all disgruntled now that I have?"

"Of course, and I'm so happy that you did," Tiffany agreed. "I love seeing you happy and I want you and Dani to get married and have a white picket fence with two-point-five children and all that, but now that leaves me single as a Pringle with no one to mingle with. Doesn't Dani have a brother you can set me up with or something?"

"No, all she has is sisters and both of them are taken. You know that."

Tiffany sighed in her usual overdramatic way that never failed to make Zoey giggle. "I suppose I'll just have to continue in these mean online dating streets since you supposedly have no one to set me up with."

She rolled her eyes, knowing exactly what Tiffany was getting at. She had shown Tiffany a picture of her brother and since then, Tiffany had hinted that she should send along his phone number so she could get to know him better. It wasn't that Zoey thought her brother and Tiffany wouldn't get along. It was that she knew Mason was a dumbass and didn't want to subject one of her closest friends to him. She loved her brother, but he wasn't exactly Mr. Relationship.

"If I set you up with my brother and he does something dumb, I don't want you blaming me for his mistakes."

"Why would I blame you for his mistakes?" Tiffany asked. "I know how to handle army guys especially. I grew up in a family full of them. You just have to know how to stroke their ego enough to give them what they want so that you can get exactly what you want. It's just a game with them. But really, they're big babies who want to be coddled."

Zoey could admit that Tiffany wasn't completely off base with her assessment. Mason was responsible but at times he did seem like he wanted to be coddled, which was always strange given the fact that he raised her. "I'll think about it," she said finally, wanting to change the subject. Mason would be in town soon enough as it was, and she had already planned to introduce him to not only her friends but also potentially Dani. It was probably too soon but when it came to making sure that Zoey wasn't reading too much into a situation like before, Mason was a good judge of that.

Tiffany rolled her eyes but nodded. "Fine, whatever. Now tell me about you and Dani. Have you said the L-word yet? Is it time to break out the U-Haul?"

Zoey shook her head. "I told you, we're taking it slow. I'm the first woman she's ever dated and I'm pretty sure she hasn't dated anyone seriously since she split with her ex-husband."

Tiffany nodded. "And you're sure she's bisexual and not just experimenting?"

It was a valid question but one she didn't want to dwell on. Their kisses didn't feel like mere experimentation, and it wasn't like Dani was trying to lay lips on her only for an audience. Zoey had dealt with that previously—girls kissing her just to interest some guy who was watching, and Dani's kisses didn't feel like that. She never shied away from her in public either like she was trying to keep their situationship on the down-low. Dani seemed happy enough to hold Zoey's hand when they met at Thomas's diner and always gave her a kiss when they parted in full view of whoever was out at the time.

"She hasn't labeled herself with me," Zoey said finally. "But I guess we can go with that. I don't want to label her as something she isn't, but I don't know where she is with working that out internally."

Tiffany nodded, though the look of suspicion stayed painted on her face. "I suppose that's true. Maybe I need to dial it up a notch and start asking my own questions during book club."

Zoey narrowed her eyes. "Questions like what? I don't want you bombarding her and making her uncomfortable, Tiff."

Tiffany waved off her words. "I wouldn't bombard her. That's not my style."

"Tiff—"

"Don't worry," she cut in. "I have a foolproof plan for tonight's book club. Just leave it to me."

Zoey worried all through the day and well into book club. Tiffany hadn't even given her a glimpse of what she might ask Dani, leaving her to worry that she should have been firm in saying no. When Tiffany had texted that she wouldn't be able to make it to book club, Zoey had tried not to seem too excited. Truthfully, she wanted answers about where this was going with Dani just as much as Tiffany did. But she was willing to be patient. She would continue showing Dani that she would make an excellent partner.

Things were underway when Dani stumbled into Zoey's place, an apology for being late on her lips. "Work ran over and then I had to wait for Ava to get home to watch Jordan for me."

Zoey smiled. "It's totally okay."

"Yeah, we understand how things can go," Sharon said with a knowing smile. "It's hard when you have a little one."

Dani's smile looked grateful, and she dropped down on the couch beside Zoey. For a moment, she turned her dark brown gaze, locking with Zoey's. It was like gravity, pulling them together as Zoey found herself leaning in. Her gaze flickered down to Dani's lips until she remembered where they were and who they were with. With a hard swallow, Zoey straightened and turned her gaze to the book in her hand.

"We haven't gotten too far in our discussion, so you should be able to hop right in." When Zoey chanced a glance back up, Dani's eyes were still on her. Movement caught Zoey's attention, and she saw Dani's fingers grip the book in her hands tighter. As if also realizing that they weren't alone, Dani finally looked away. Her fingers were graceful as they parted the pages, spreading the book open to the page marked with her bookmark.

"Perfect," Dani replied, her voice soft in a way that sent shivers through Zoey's body. "I'm really enjoying this book so far."

"Me too," Sharon spoke up, further jolting Zoey out of whatever moment she had fallen into. *Get it together*, she thought, frantically forcing herself to focus back on the chapters chosen for tonight's discussion. A quick glance around confirmed that everyone else was equally enthralled in the book, and she sighed in relief that no one remarked on the tension-filled exchange she and Dani had just had. When Dani leaned into her, Zoey smiled softly soaking in her warmth as their arms pressed together. She wasn't sure if anyone besides Tiffany would get the significance of this, but Zoey could feel her cheeks heat up. It didn't stop her from leaning into Dani as the discussion about their book for the month continued.

Zoey added comments, enjoying each time the conversation went on a tangent, but a good portion of her time was spent stealing glances. There was something different in the way Dani held herself today. There was something a bit more muted that she wanted to get to the bottom of. Zoey leaned over, hoping that her voice wouldn't be overheard.

"Is everything okay?"

Dani looked at her in surprise. "Yeah, everything is fine. Why do you ask?"

Zoey shrugged. "You seem tired. You're more than welcome to take a break if you need."

Dani turned a grin at her. "And miss seeing you? No

way. I'll be fine." Dani sounded sure that she was okay, and Zoey only smiled and nodded. It wasn't until book club was wrapping up that she realized Dani had fallen completely asleep. Her head was hanging low as she leaned more heavily into Zoey.

"Poor thing. She must be exhausted," Sharon said as she collected the empty plates and cups. "Being a single mom is no joke."

Zoey nodded as she looked down at Dani. "I can only imagine."

"Maybe if you don't have to go anywhere, you can let her nap for a bit here. I'm sure she would appreciate it."

"You are absolutely right," Zoey agreed. "I'll see you next week, same time same place, yes?"

"Wouldn't miss it for the world."

When everyone else had left, Zoey slowly approached Dani, moving quietly not to wake her up. She didn't want to seem creepy, but as she gazed down at her, she couldn't help but note how relaxed Dani looked in sleep. She had noticed the slightly glassy gaze when Dani had walked in. She'd looked exhausted and if not for Zoey selfishly wanting to spend time with her, she would have suggested Dani go home and get some rest.

"I should have just told her to go home," Zoey said quietly as she reached out. She grabbed the blanket she kept on the back of the couch and pulled it over Dani's shoulders. When her hand brushed over her shoulder, Dani sighed softly and shifted, turning into the touch. It was such a small move and yet to Zoey, it was everything.

That Dani felt comfortable enough to fall asleep here, with her, meant a lot. She knew she should be more casual about this. Falling fast and hard was a thing for her that too often blew up in her face. They were too entwined for her to go into this without considering everything.

Still, Zoey couldn't deny that she was enjoying the direction things had been going in. Even with Holly, they had never really enmeshed themselves in such a way that had her feeling completely comfortable. Before Zoey could figure out what to do next, her cellphone rang, and she quickly moved to answer so the sound didn't wake Dani up. She rolled her eyes when she saw it was Tiffany.

"After worrying me all day, I can't believe you texted that you weren't coming and didn't even give a reason. I thought you wanted to ask all the questions?"

"I did," Tiffany insisted. "But my car decided tonight was the perfect time for a flat and I was on that back road near the cemetery that has shit cell service, so I was only able to send a couple texts. Thankfully, the one to Aiden went through so I could get him to tow me to the shop. But, a little birdie told me that you and the delightful Dani are now all alone in your cozy little condo."

Zoey knew that word traveled fast in small towns, but this was ridiculous. "Seriously? Everyone only left like five minutes ago."

"And that's five minutes you could be using to put the moves on the sexy single mama."

"Then why did you call me?" Zoey asked, hissing out her words.

"Because," Tiffany replied, drawing out her syllables. "I just got word that the state board is considering our request to have a second full-time librarian on a permanent basis and not just on contract."

Zoey froze. That wasn't what she was expecting to hear. She had known that Tiffany was working on securing funding for staff, and she of course knew that Tiffany wanted her to stay in Peach Blossom. But small-town libraries were often overlooked when it came to budgets. The only reason Zoey could even afford to just be a contractor instead of a full-time employee was because she had her own benefits, a second larger cash flow and, truthfully, a trust from her late parents. It had helped that college had been funded by her trust, leaving her with no debt even after getting a master's degree.

"Are you still there?"

"Yeah," Zoey said quickly, covering for her silence. "That's amazing. I know you were worried about that."

"No, I was worried about losing you. There's a difference," Tiffany said. "Now, we still have a few weeks before we find out if it's approved or if I have to sell my nonexistent firstborn to put it through again next month, but if it is, I want you with us. Permanently."

It meant a lot for Zoey to hear those words. There were so many emotions running through her that she didn't even know what to say. Peach Blossom had grown on her and even with how small it was compared to places she had previously lived, she never found herself feeling like she was missing out. She hadn't once felt the need to get up and leave, to drive down the highway looking for another place to feel like home. As she looked down at where Dani slept, she was cautiously optimistic about the fact that she felt she could be happy here.

"I know it's a lot to ask," Tiffany continued. "Peach Blossom doesn't have as much going for it like a larger city with a wider net of libraries."

Tiffany wasn't wrong and yet she was at the same time. It had taken years of therapy for Zoey to understand how much she wanted to find a place to belong; where she felt she could be herself and fit in without forcing it. She enjoyed traveling with her brother, or rather, she liked seeing new things and discovering new places, but they had never had a home base, and she'd hated that. It always left her feeling like her life was built on sand, able to be blown away with the gentlest of breezes.

"No," Zoey said finally. She looked down at Dani's sleeping face. "Peach Blossom has a lot more going for it than you all realize."

Tiffany was quiet for a moment before she spoke again. "What makes you say that?"

Zoey thought about how to put it into words. She had moved here on a whim, the need for research and the invitation from a friend. She wouldn't have heard of Peach Blossom otherwise. But as she talked with people in town, some who could trace their roots back generations, she found a sort of stability and steadfastness that spoke to her on a level she was still trying to understand.

"Just, everything," Zoey said finally. She brushed her

fingers across Dani's cheek. "I can see why you wanted to come back after we graduated. Peach Blossom is really something special."

Thirteen

Exhausted.

Dani had been more than a little of that when she had pulled out of the parking lot at work. She probably should have headed home and apologized to Zoey for missing this week's book club, but after pulling a couple double shifts, she was in desperate need of that familiar energizing smile to brighten her day. It explained why she had booked it to Zoey's place, but it didn't explain why when she opened her eyes, she was seeing the world horizontally.

The living room was familiar with the wall of books that still made her eyes widen in awe every time she saw them, but the angle was definitely not.

"Are you okay?"

The pillow underneath her head shifted, and with a start, Dani realized she wasn't lying on a pillow at all. Her head was resting on one of Zoey's thighs and when she looked up, she saw Zoey holding a book. Dani had been in this exact position a few times, but with her being used as a pillow by Jordan or, when they were much younger, her sisters. She couldn't remember the last time she had been the one resting like this, enjoying the closeness and sense of comfort this position brought. It was novel in a way that had Dani wishing she hadn't been caught awake. How strange it was that she felt so comfortable with someone she had only known for a few months.

Dani looked around, surprised when she realized the reason the room was so quiet was because she and Zoey were the only ones left. She lifted her arm and looked at her watch, noting the time.

"Book club is over?" she asked, her voice still rough from sleep. She shifted, turning over to take the strain off her neck as she looked up at Zoey. "Sorry. I didn't mean to fall asleep."

Zoey shook her head with a smile that looked so soft and touchable that Dani's fingers twitched with the need to reach out. "It's totally fine. We all saw you were sleepy. And besides, your little snores were adorable. They added character to the discussion."

Dani widened her eyes. "I didn't snore, did I?"

Zoey shrugged. "Just a few little quiet ones." When she made a soft noise pretending to snore, Dani huffed out a soft laugh.

"That does not sound like me."

"Oh?" Zoey asked as she closed her book and sat it

down on the couch beside her. "So, your snores are much louder?"

"If you're lucky, maybe you'll find out." Dani didn't realize what she said until the words were out there, but she found she didn't want to take them back. They had been flirting more, dancing around subjects to music only they could hear. Dani had worries she would be rusty in this, but she'd found it easy to fall into heated words with her. Zoey, whose shyness only seemed to be a front for her masterful way with words. Sometimes, Dani just sat back and marveled at how she weaved them like magic in the air.

"Didn't I tell you; I was born on a lucky day!" Zoey said, her smile morphing to a smirk that had Dani wide-awake. They hadn't gone beyond kissing and occasionally holding hands, but Dani would be lying if she said she wasn't itching for more. She had talked more with Ava and Vini, wanting to make sure she wasn't seeing signs that weren't actually there. A few times, they had chastised her for thinking things were so remarkably different than dating men.

If you want to kiss her, just say so. If she likes you as much as it seems she does, I doubt she'd say no.

It had been good advice, and Dani had done her best to take it to heart. When it came to the idea of taking things further, Dani was surprised to find she was more eagerly excited than apprehensive. She'd tried doing some research when everyone was out of the house, but was annoyed to find how unrealistic a lot of it looked. She'd damn near pulled a muscle just watching some of the videos that popped up during her search, and figured the production of it all was the same on both sides of the house, straight and lesbian. She'd just do what she always did, wing it or ask questions.

"Are you trying to let me know you're hoping to get lucky?" Dani didn't look away as Zoey seemed to think about her question. She knew it hadn't been long since they started seeing each other and they were taking things slowly, but damn if Dani didn't want to speed some things up. Those damn cardigans, as cute as they were, hid the fact that Zoey had body for days. Her legs were shapely, leading up to hips that made Dani want to reach out and grab them. And her waist called to Dani. She hadn't even been concerned about liking Zoey sexually once she realized that every time previous wasn't just a look of admiration. Being self-aware was doing wonders for reshaping Dani's world view.

"Always," Zoey breathed out. As if realizing what she said, she blinked quickly and backtracked. "But I mean, we don't have to do anything of course. I know this is newer for you."

They'd briefly talked about Dani's lack of experience with women a couple nights ago when kissing had led to Zoey under Dani on this very couch. She had wanted to go further, but had been struck silent by no idea how to get there. When she'd explained to Zoey, she'd expected some jokes or maybe, at worst, for her to say thanks but no thanks. But instead, Zoey had backed off and asked questions. That had blown Dani's mind, and nearly blown her resolve to go slow. Who knew that asking sexual questions could have led to being so turned on that she needed to leave before she broke her resolve.

Now though, Dani was feeling good. She wasn't worried about putting on a show. She just wanted to make Zoey feel even half as good as she made her feel. Before she could lose her nerve, Dani reached up and brushed her fingers over Zoey's cheek.

"I know we don't have to," she replied, voice going softer as she looked into Zoey's eyes. "But what if I want to?"

Zoey reached up and cupped the back of Dani's hand, and nuzzled into her palm. Behind her glasses, her dark brown eyes went molten, and Dani marveled at the switch. This Zoey was a siren drawing her in with ease.

"Then I want to."

Zoey had barely gotten her words out before Dani had pulled her lips down to meet. The kiss was unlike the ones they'd traded before. Those had been almost exploratory as if they were both feeling each other out. This one was all consuming. Zoey's lips moved against hers with a hunger only matched by Dani's own. The position wasn't the most comfortable, but Dani didn't move. She didn't want to break the molten spell they'd fallen prey to.

Zoey's hand squeezed hers before another cupped the back of Dani's neck, propping her head up and taking the strain off her neck. It was that consideration that had Dani groaning into their kiss. It was the catalyst that finally had her shifting up and over until she straddled Zoey's lap, giving her more freedom to kiss harder and deeper. This hunger in her was new and she delighted in how readily it was accepted and channeled back. Nothing about this was light or dainty. This was an all-consuming need to imprint herself onto Zoey's very soul. Dani felt needy, like a thirst she hadn't been aware of was finally being fulfilled.

"If it's too much," she panted out when they briefly broke apart for air. "Tell me to stop and I will."

Zoey shook her head before gripping the back of her locs and reeling her in again. "Don't stop."

Dani's smile was buried between their lips as they kissed again. She could feel the hard edge of Zoey's book scraping against her knee, but even that wasn't enough to move her to stop. Her hands roamed, brushing over and down Zoey's back, only stopping when the cushions of the couch blocked her path. Zoey's hands gripped at Dani's thighs hard enough that she wondered if she might catch glimpses of finger-shaped bruises later. The thought of having something physical on her skin to remember this by was another layer of herself being unlocked and she filed it away to come back to later.

"Maybe we should move to your bed," Dani whispered before placing sucking kisses down Zoey's chin. She tilted her head back with a soft whine.

"Are you sure?" she asked, her throat bobbing as she swallowed. "I don't want to push you for too much if you aren't ready."

Dani chuckled, enjoying the way it made Zoey shiver. She couldn't help but keep going to one spot on Zoey's neck that smelled divine.

"Does it feel like I'm not ready?"

"No, but…" Zoey trailed off as she sucked in a sharp breath. Dani soothed the bit of skin she had just nibbled with a flick of her tongue. "Fuck. You taste perfect."

"Jesus," Zoey wheezed out. "How didn't you know you liked women?"

Dani shook her head before darting her tongue out to brush over the shell of her ear. "I was busy. And maybe I was waiting for you."

Zoey's hands shot out, gripping her cheeks before crushing their lips back together. When they came up for air again, Zoey's eyes were half-lidded and full of heat. "You can't just say shit like that to me."

She groaned before gripping Zoey's waist.

"Do that again."

"What?" Zoey asked, nose scrunching when she frowned in clear confusion.

"Curse. Say *shit* again," Dani said. "Something about you being so sweet and cursing gets me going."

Zoey's eyes widened before she narrowed them again and smirked. "I'm not as sweet as you think."

"Fuck. Okay. Bedroom," Dani said, throwing her hands off so she could move to stand. "I need you naked when you say things like that to me."

Zoey quickly moved to follow but reached out to grab Dani's arm again, pressing her against the wall and diving in for more kisses. They moved in stops and starts, trading places against the walls. At one point, they nearly tripped over each other's feet and when both of them broke down into giggles, Dani couldn't help but marvel at how easy it all was. She wanted Zoey with a fervor that surprised even her, but even more than that, she was having fun. It wasn't that sex hadn't been fun before, but there had always been an undercurrent of her needing to perform. She felt none of that here. She wanted to touch and explore the similarities and the differences between their bodies.

Right when they crossed the threshold of Zoey's room, a shrill sound broke out. Zoey frowned but Dani groaned in annoyance and rested her head back on the doorframe. She knew that ringtone. Nothing good ever came from it blaring out from her phone.

"Damn it," she said before lifting her head and looking at Zoey. "I need to answer that. It's Jordan's dad and he rarely calls me when it's Jordan's time with him."

She didn't look upset as Dani leaned forward, giving her a soft peck in apology. "It's okay. Go ahead and grab your phone. I'll wait for you in here, okay?"

Dani nodded with a grateful smile. "Perfect. I'll only be a minute."

Separating from Zoey took everything in her and if not for the fact that Jordan was with his dad, she would've ignored the phone completely. Dani walked back into the living room. She quickly found her purse and grabbed her phone, answering it before the ringing stopped.

"What, Jacob?"

"Mom?"

Dani stood straighter when she heard Jordan's voice. "Jordan? Why are you calling from your dad's phone? Is everything alright?" She heard him sniffle before he spoke again.

"No. Can you come get me?"

Dani nodded though she knew he couldn't see her. She hurried back to the bedroom. "Yes, of course I can come get you. I'll be there in just a bit, okay?" She saw Zoey look up at her. "Tell your dad I'm on my way, okay?"

"Okay. I will."

Dani looked down at the phone after Jordan hung up. "I'm so sorry, Zoey. That was Jordan and he sounds upset."

She shook her head. "Don't apologize. It's okay. Let me help you find your things."

Dani tried not to let her anxiety show as she found her keys and put on her shoes. She was worried. Rarely did Jordan call her to pick him up early from his dad's. They had a set schedule that only had a few deviations when necessary. That he called sounding this upset was enough to have her not bothering to lace up her shoes.

When she gathered everything, she turned to Zoey with an apologetic expression. "I really am sorry. I didn't mean to get you turned on, only to leave you with blue balls and dip."

Zoey smiled and shook her head. "First of all, blue balls

aren't a thing. And second, you're a mom. I understand that Jordan comes first. It's totally okay."

Her words loosened something in Dani's chest, and she pulled Zoey in, kissing her softly. "Thank you."

Zoey's smile was soft as she nodded. "Go. Make sure Jordan's okay and I'll talk to you later."

Dani nodded turning away before she was tempted to apologize again.

Fourteen

Jordan slammed into the house and if it were any other night, Dani would have said something. As it was, she could understand his anger, considering when she had gotten to his dad's house to pick him up, he was already sitting out on the front stoop with his overnight bag packed. If not for trying to maintain her peace, she would have marched her ass into the house and demanded to know why their son was sitting outside in the dark by himself. Instead, Dani had taken a few deep breaths, grabbed Jordan's bag and hurried him to the car.

The drive home had been quiet, and she pretended not to see the dried tear tracks on his cheeks. Dani was happy that he felt comfortable enough to call her and tell her to come get him, but he hadn't responded to any of her questions. After the third one was answered by silence, Dani decided to give it a rest until they got to the house.

When they walked in the front door, the house was

quiet. Dani knew Ava was out at Grace's. She figured their dad was in his room watching television, and she didn't want to get into why she was home earlier than the norm or why Jordan was here when he was supposed to be at his dad's house until next week. She figured the fewer people around when she tried to get him to open up and talk about what happened, the better.

"Why don't you go on upstairs and get showered and then I'll be up in just a minute, okay?"

Jordan's fists clenched and Dani waited to see if he was going to say anything. After a moment, he just nodded sharply before grabbing his bag and stomping up the stairs. She walked into the kitchen and grabbed a cup before pouring herself a glass of water. Her body was still thrumming from not only the adrenaline of picking up Jordan but also exhaustion and the slightest bit of arousal. It was a strange mix that she wasn't used to, and she needed a few minutes to collect herself before she could switch completely into mommy mode. When she heard footsteps, she turned in time to see her dad walk into the kitchen.

"Why does it sound like a herd of wildebeest are stamping their way upstairs?" He gave her a once-over. "And why are you back home so early?"

Dani sighed before setting the cup on the kitchen counter. "I wasn't planning on it, but Jordan called me and asked me to come pick him up from his dad's house early."

He raised an eyebrow and looked up at the ceiling before back at her. "He asked you to come pick him up a whole four days earlier? What the hell happened for him to do that?"

Dani shrugged, though it was more out of frustration than nonchalance. "I'm not sure and he wouldn't talk about it when we were in the car. I told him to go upstairs and shower and that I would come up to see what's going on when he was done." She crossed her arms and looked away. "That man had my baby sitting out on the front porch with his bag when I pulled up."

"Oh. I'm sure it took everything in you not to go inside and raise hell, am I right?" When she nodded, he chuckled softly and shook his head. "Sometimes I wonder if that man has a death wish."

"I don't wonder if that man has a death wish, I know he does." When Dani heard the water turn on upstairs, she dropped her arms and leaned back against the kitchen counter. "Sometimes, I'm wondering if things would have been better had I made some different decisions."

"Different decisions?" her dad asked. "You mean different decisions about who you decided to lie with?"

Dani looked at him sharply, wondering if he was talking about Jacob or if he knew about her and Zoey. She genuinely liked Zoey as a person and even though they hadn't yet gone public with their relationship, they also weren't hiding it either. It was the same balancing act Dani had always done when it came to dating. She wasn't about to have a conversation with her dad or Jordan about it just yet, not when things were so new. No, he had to be talking about her marriage with Jacob. She decided to go with that and keep things with Zoey quiet for now. Peach Blossom was a small enough town anyway that people would find out soon enough if they hadn't suspected already.

"That among other decisions," Dani said finally. "I don't know what goes on in that man's head sometimes. It's like he doesn't even try when it comes to Jordan, and I don't know how much longer I can keep propping up this relationship. But I know if I don't keep at it, that I'll be labeled as the bad guy for not facilitating the two of them spending time together."

Daniel nodded before walking over to the dining table and sitting down. He pulled out the chair beside him and patted it, gesturing for Dani to join him. She followed his lead, collapsing down into the chair as if the weight of not only the current situation but also her exhaustion fell to her shoulders.

"I know it feels like sometimes you're doggy paddling against a rough current," Daniel said. "If you haven't heard it lately, I want you to know that I think you're doing an excellent job raising Jordan and really keeping this entire household running."

Dani knew it, but it was still good to hear. "Thanks, Pop. But now I need to figure out what's going on with Jordan and if it's even something that I can fix."

Daniel nodded. "I get that, but you also need to try to come to terms with the fact that you might not be able to fix this. It's not always up to you to fix something you weren't the one to break."

That idea sounded good in theory, but Dani didn't really know how to utilize it in practice. If there was something going on with Jordan, she had to be the one to fix it because if she didn't, who would? Jacob had taken a back seat when it came to Jordan, even right after he was born and none of that changed when the two of them had split. Dani had hoped that when Jacob got a new girlfriend, something in him would shift and he would realize that he needed to be a better person for his son. That idea had quickly been dashed and Dani had reevaluated her dependence on him doing what needed to be done.

"And about making different decisions," Daniel continued, giving her a look. "I think 'everything happening for a reason' is a terrible phrase. People said that to me back when your mom first died, and it made me want to deck them. But knowing that, I do think that we go through certain things in life in order to prepare us for what comes next."

"What do you mean?" Dani asked, not understanding where he was going with this.

"I think with everything that had gone on years ago, if you had met Zoey then, you wouldn't have been ready for her now."

Dani really shouldn't have been surprised that her dad knew about Zoey, which meant the whole town definitely knew about them at this point. She figured the start of it was probably Sharon. She wasn't exactly known for keeping her mouth shut when it came to town gossip and if she paid half as close attention to Dani and Zoey's interactions during book club as she did to the books they were reading, then she had no doubt observed them sharing significant looks more than once. Maybe even a hand brush or two.

"Did you or Mom ever have an idea that I might be interested in women?"

He sat back and gave her a considering look. "Honestly, I don't know if your mother ever suspected it, sweetheart. I don't know if I ever really thought about it either. We tended to just let you girls come to us when you had things you needed to say."

That sounded about right. Dani had only been a little apprehensive when she first came to them to let them know that she was pregnant with Jordan. She had known it would be an uncomfortable conversation, but she hadn't even considered hiding it. When it came to coming out of the closet, Ava and Vini had come to her first before going to talk to their parents. Secrets in their household didn't stay buried for long.

"Sometimes I think I should know myself better, considering I'm about to turn thirty."

Her dad's laughter was loud, leaving Dani feeling some type of way about it. "Oh, don't give me that look, sugar. I know you young ones have this idea in your head that by the time you reach some arbitrary age you should know everything about yourself, but I just want to let you know that that is not real. Hell, I'm damn near sixty and I'm still figuring things out about myself."

Despite his words, Dani still felt a little annoyed that

she had missed this big part of herself and slightly ashamed that it had taken her this long for it to come to fruition. "I get that, I guess, but it still just seems like I'm starting out behind."

The water upstairs shut off and Dani glanced up at the ceiling, knowing that she needed to get up there and have a conversation with Jordan. Her dad's hand brushed hers. "There's no such thing as having to start on page one, sweetheart. Sometimes, chapter one happens after the book has already begun."

Dani looked up again when she heard Jordan call her from his room. Daniel patted her hand again.

"Go. I'll turn the lights off down here and then I'm headed to bed myself." They stood and impulsively, Dani wrapped her arms around her dad, hugging him in a way she hadn't in a long time. When his arms curled around her, drawing her in, she felt the type of comfort that had always given her strength when she was a kid. She had been named after her dad, but this was the first time in a long time that she truly felt the connection that his namesake brought.

"Thanks, Pop."

He brushed a kiss over her forehead. "Anytime, kiddo."

Dani took that comfort and strength with her as she walked up the stairs to Jordan's room. She was happy that Ava was out, and Vini was out of the country, so there wouldn't be any interruptions. She would probably fill them in later on, but for now, it was just her and Jordan.

When Dani got to his door, she knocked softly and called out to him.

"Hey, kiddo. You ready for me to come in?"

"Yeah," Jordan replied, his voice muffled from behind the closed door. Dani pushed it open slowly, just in case he wanted to change his mind. When she saw him, he was sitting on his bed, towel wrapped around his shoulders and in a pair of oversize basketball shorts. His chin was on his knees, and he had wrapped his hands around his shins, hiding his face. Everything about him screamed that he was not okay, and Dani closed the door behind her, giving them privacy so they could talk. She gave him a minute as she walked over and sat down beside him on the bed.

"Are you ready to talk about what's going on?" she asked, pitching her voice softly as not to startle him. She wasn't surprised when he didn't lift his head.

"Dad's getting married." Jordan's voice was still muffled but Dani heard him clearly. She schooled her face to hide her shock. She had known that eventually this day would come but she wasn't expecting to find out about it from Jordan. She and Jacob had always had an agreement that when they started dating someone seriously, they would let each other know. It was an agreement that held when he started dating his most recent girlfriend— or she guessed she should say *fiancée*. The only reason she hadn't brought up Zoey was because it was still new, and they hadn't had the serious talk that Dani felt they needed to have before making such a big decision.

She figured it would also be different because technically Zoey and Jordan had already met in some capac-
ity. But she wasn't going to be a hypocrite and introduce
her to Jordan as her significant other without having the
conversation with Jacob first. Or, she hadn't planned to.
Maybe she could reconsider things, given the fact that
she was the only one seemingly playing by the rules that
they had set together years ago.

"I can see how that would be upsetting," she said gently. Dani had always tried to be diplomatic in her discussion of Jacob around Jordan. Even if she wanted to curse
his name, she kept it PG and saved that for the group
chat or when she knew Jordan was nowhere in listening distance.

Jordan lifted his head and glanced over at Dani. His
eyes were red rimmed and still shiny with unshed tears. It
tore at Dani's heartstrings to see him so upset, especially
considering he had been around Jacob's now fiancée for
the past few years. There had to be something more he
wasn't telling her for him to be having this visceral of a
reaction to something that was honestly probably inevitable. Dani didn't expect Jacob to stay single or unmar-
ried for his entire life. She didn't really expect much from
him these days as it was.

"I thought you liked Evelyn," Dani said. She reached
out and ran a hand through Jordan's curls, hoping the familiar touch would help soothe him into explaining more
about what his issues truly were with this news. "Were
you two not getting along?"

Jordan shook his head before lifting it fully and drop-ping his feet back on the floor. Dani took it as a good sign that he was no longer curled up, as if trying to pro-tect himself from blows. "She's fine. It's just that I didn't know that she was pregnant too."

That threw her for an even bigger loop. Why the hell would Jacob throw that information on Jordan all at once? Hell, she was an adult with no residual feelings for Jacob and even she was thrown for a loop. As much as Jordan seemed like a well-spoken and mature kid, he was still just that: a kid. He required a little more consideration before just dropping bits of news on him.

"Ah," Dani intoned. "I see how that would be rough. It's a lot of information to throw at you, kiddo. But I'm sure your dad thought you would be excited for them."

Jordan looked at her as if she had said the most ridicu-lous thing in the world, and Dani knew she was missing something vital. "Did you know?"

She shook her head. "No, I had no idea."

"What about the fact that they're naming the baby Jacob?"

Oh, fuck. Dani didn't know how to take that. She knew that Jacob had always wanted to name a child after him-self, similar to how Dani was named after her dad. But to do it after they already had a child seemed like an ass-hole idea, considering Jordan had no idea what was going down to begin with. When Dani didn't immediately re-spond, Jordan took up his previous position curling in on himself and closing away from the world. It hurt Dani to see him like this, but she wasn't sure what else to say.

"Jordan, you know your dad loves you," she said, thinking quickly. "I'm sure he didn't announce that to hurt you."

"Can I have some time by myself?" Jordan asked softly. Dani had to strain her hearing just to hear him. She wanted to say no. She wanted to make him talk more so she could understand exactly where his head was at, but she had always prided herself on giving Jordan space when asked. She wanted him to feel comfortable coming to her and that meant not pushing all the time. She had to pick and choose her battles with him, and this was a battle that she knew she needed more information to win.

She nodded, though he wasn't looking at her, before wrapping her arms around him in a tight hug and kissing his forehead like her dad had done for her.

"I'll just be in my room so don't hesitate to come get me if you need me, okay?"

Jordan nodded but didn't say anything else. With a heavy heart, Dani dropped her arms and stood up from the bed. She walked to his door, glancing back at him, her heart hurting at the way that he clung to himself. She wanted to go back, grab him and pick him up like she had when he was a toddler and hurt himself. But just like everything else, the change in their dynamic was inevitable. She opened the door and left his room, closing it softly behind her. She had some calls to make.

Fifteen

It had been two days since Zoey had seen Dani. They had texted a little, but the messages had been short and generic, totally unlike the days before Dani had to leave abruptly in the middle of the night. Zoey wanted to reach out and see if everything was okay and if she could help in any way, but she wasn't sure if that was crossing the lines they had sort of set when they fell into this relationship. There was also the part where she hoped Jordan was okay. He hadn't shown up to the esports league yesterday, which was unusual for him. She had casually asked about him, but his friends hadn't had any additional information, only stating that he hadn't been at school that day. Zoey was more than a little worried and a whole lot confused. She didn't think she had done anything to warrant the lack of communication, but she still couldn't help but worry.

The workday passed slowly and by the time Zoey was walking through her front door, she was exhausted and just wanted to lounge on the couch with her most recent read. She had been making good progress on her manuscript, enough to take a break for the night. That came in handy on a night like this when she didn't want to do anything other than wallow and think herself into circles. Her phone ringing broke her calm and she sighed when she answered.

"Hey, sis. Checking in to see how you're doing."

Mason's timing was a bit rough, but Zoey knew she should take advantage of him having time to call. She wasn't always able to reach him when she wanted to, and the past couple weeks hadn't been any different.

"About as well as can be expected when I'm on a deadline that is drawing ever closer," she replied before leaning back against the couch. "How's Arizona?"

"Hot as fuck and everything wants to kill me. Things are moving a bit ahead of schedule, so I'm actually thinking about dropping in early to see you on my way to my next stop."

That wasn't unusual. Mason often crashed with her for a couple weeks before he packed up and moved on to his next station, and sometimes his schedule changed abruptly leaving them to scramble a bit. This time though, he had hinted that he would be doing another stint overseas instead of staying stateside. The last time they had talked, he had been cagey about where he was going to potentially be relocated, and Zoey could only hope it wasn't somewhere too dangerous.

"That's totally fine," she replied. "Tiffany is excited to

meet you finally. I think she has this vision of a cool army guy in her head. I keep telling her to lower her standards since you're just a massive weirdo."

Mason's laughter was booming, and it never failed to make Zoey smile. This time was no different. She wasn't completely lying. Mason was a dork through and through. The two of them were fairly similar but they just expressed their weirdness by being into slightly different vices. Zoey collected books. Mason collected LEGO sets. If the man ever decided to sell his sets, she didn't doubt that he could fund a small country.

"Nothing wrong with a little hero worship," he replied, drawing her attention back to him. "Besides, I'm about as normal as it gets in the army. You want to see weirdos? I'll introduce you to some of the new recruits."

"No thanks."

"We have some new women in too. I know they would be much more palatable."

Zoey snorted and shook her head. Her brother always joked about having a soldier he wanted her to meet. She knew he was joking, but she figured it was as good a lead as any into the change in her life.

"Actually, I wouldn't be interested in any of them because I've met someone. Here, in Peach Blossom."

Mason was silent for a moment. "You have. Really? I thought you said there wasn't anyone th—wait." He cut himself off. "There was someone you talked about. But I remember you saying you didn't know if they liked women."

Zoey internally kicked herself. She had talked a bit about Dani before, and with Mason's steel-trap memory, she knew he would start recalling all the conversations they had about her. "Yeah, well, turns out she does."

Mason hummed before speaking. "Are you sure? You seemed pretty adamant that you had a crush that wouldn't lead to anything. What changed?"

Zoey looked at the ceiling as she thought back to the changes that had happened over the past couple weeks. "Well, we started talking and she joined my book club. I asked her out to the movies, and we've been hanging out ever since."

"Hanging out? Have you two...you know..." Mason trailed off, sounding as awkward as they both no doubt felt.

"Why the hell would I tell you that?" Zoey couldn't help the shrillness of her voice. It wasn't like they hadn't talked about sex before. Mason raised her. He was the one who'd given her the abridged version of the birds and the bees when she was in middle school. Still, they didn't talk much about sex now that they were both adults outside of the general "don't make me an aunt too soon" jokes that she gave him whenever he flitted off to some new location.

"I don't know," Mason countered. "I'm just trying to be supportive. Jeez."

Zoey shook her head, fondness coating her exasperation. "I know, but the answer is no. We haven't done... that."

"Well, hell, sis. If you can't say the word *sex*, then you have no business having it."

"I can say the word *sex*, moron." Zoey stood up and walked into her kitchen. She loved Mason, but talking to him on an empty stomach and fully sober was a test in patience. The man drove her up the wall on a good day. "But I'm the first woman Dani's dated, so we're taking things slow. Plus, she has her son, Jordan, to consider."

Mason was quiet as Zoey pulled out a half-empty pizza box from the fridge. She grabbed a couple cold slices and tossed them on a plate. It was until the microwave was going that Mason spoke again.

"This isn't another Holly incident, is it?"

At the name of her ex-friend and pseudo girlfriend, Zoey froze. It's not that she never thought she would have to hear that name again, but it was just jarring coming from Mason. Zoey had kept everything that had been going on between her and Holly a secret until the stress had gotten too hard for her to handle alone. By the time Mason stepped in, Zoey had been damn near a wreck and ready to launch herself out of the dating pool altogether.

"Dani is nothing like Holly, Mason." Zoey wasn't sure how to explain it, but she just knew that the two women weren't even comparable. Dani hadn't tried to hide Zoey away, and whenever they had gotten caught kissing outside the diner, Dani had remained where she was instead of jumping away as if she were guilty of something. That would have sent Holly into a tailspin, where she would have ignored any and all of Zoey's attempts at communication for at least a week, leaving her wondering what she had done wrong. Embarrassingly, it had taken Zoey months to notice the pattern.

"How do you know?" Mason asked. "You're the first woman she's dated. She has a kid. Was she also married before?"

Zoey pursed her lips, not wanting to respond. She knew what Mason was driving at, but she refused to believe what had happened was repeating itself now. But, she also couldn't lie to him. If things worked out the way she hoped, he would find out eventually anyway.

"Yes."

Mason's sigh was loud and carried across the line. "Zoey…"

"It's not the same situation, Mason. I promise."

"Well, what about your author thing? Does she support you in that? Or does she talk about you getting a real job?"

Zoey winced. "She…doesn't know." She continued on when she heard Mason's sound of frustration. "Not because I don't want her to, but because I'm apparently one of her favorite authors."

"That still doesn't explain why you haven't told her," he insisted. "If you two are really trying to be in a relationship, shouldn't you talk about the things you do for work? Doesn't she wonder what you do besides hang out in the library?"

"We have talked about things, I just haven't mentioned that."

"Why the hell does she think you moved to her town

then?" Mason asked. "Most people aren't moving to small towns in Georgia when they have the option to go practically anywhere else."

"Hey, I like Peach Blossom. This town has been good to me and so have the people."

He scoffed. "So good that you've been hiding things from them. That does not instill confidence, Zo."

"I'm not hiding myself, Mason. I slipped up when we first met and didn't tell her, so now I'm trying to find the right time to bring it up. That's all. There's nothing more to it than that." Zoey could hear the frustration in her voice, and it irked her that she was now having to defend her choices.

"Zoey," he began, his voice dropping into that tone that she hated. It was his parental voice, and it always made her feel like a child. "When was the last time you talked to your therapist?"

"Mason, stop. I don't need to talk to my therapist about this. I know Dani and Holly are two separate people. The relationships are not the same."

"I'm not saying that," Mason insisted. "I'm just saying, you have this need for family, and I get it, okay? I sometimes feel the same way. But that means we have to make sure that we aren't seeing something that isn't there just to feed that need."

Zoey hated when he got like this, because often he was right. She did want the perfect stable family that she and Mason hadn't gotten when they were younger. She knew that she had overlooked several red flags during her time with Holly, but she wasn't seeing those now with Dani. They both were single, divorced moms but that was where the similarities ended.

"When are you coming?" Zoey asked him.

"Don't change the subject."

"I'm not trying to," she insisted. "I want to try to set up a time for you to meet Dani so you can see that things are different."

"I'll hold you to that. I'll send you my flight information as soon as I finalize it." Zoey heard muffled voices come across the phone line and she figured he was being called away. "Love you, Zo. Be careful and I'll see you soon."

The phone disconnected before she had a chance to respond, and she shook her head when she looked down at it. Mason had given her some things to think about and as much as she wanted to push the questions away, she knew he was bringing them up for good reason. Zoey didn't have the best track record when it came to her own sense of self-preservation and relationships. Then there was the matter of whether or not the board would approve the budget to hire her on permanently. Peach Blossom was starting to feel like home, but Zoey was still in limbo about whether or not she would be able to keep it or if in a little over six months from now, when her library contract was up and her book was done, it would all just be a distant memory.

Sixteen

Dani looked down at her phone and winced when she sent her latest text message to Zoey. She wasn't avoiding her per se, but the past week had been a test in patience. The night she picked Jordan up early, she had tried to talk to Jacob, but he hadn't picked up any of her calls. She'd left him a voicemail and texted, but both remained unanswered. Jordan had taken a couple days off from school before returning a few days ago, and Dani had taken the days as sick days to stay with him in case he decided he was ready to talk. Most of the time, Jordan had stayed in his room. Dani had checked on him a couple times and he'd either been huddled in bed or on his computer. Daniel had gone in once or twice to talk to him, and Dani had had to curb her jealousy when she heard the faint murmur of their voices.

There was a time when she was the main one Jordan reached for when he felt big emotions. It was hard to have that change now, right when she wanted to be there for him the most. It also meant she wasn't being the most attentive to Zoey. After spending a good amount of time together over the past week, it was strange to Dani to not have seen her or at least gotten lunch together, however brief. Even now, Zoey had texted, inviting Dani to Thomas's diner for a quick bite, and Dani had hated to turn her down. What if she were gone and Jordan decided he wanted to talk to her? As far as she knew, Jacob hadn't reached out to him, and Dani didn't feel right just abandoning Jordan now.

"What are you doing, sitting down here by yourself on a Saturday?" Daniel asked when he walked into the kitchen. Dani was sitting at the table, a now-lukewarm cup of tea cupped in her hands. She had come down to relax and think on what she was supposed to do next, but she'd gotten caught up in her own spiraling thoughts that led nowhere.

"Just thinking," she replied finally. She lifted the cup, taking a small sip. "How was the talk with Jordan?"

Daniel smiled knowingly before coming over to take a seat. "Oh, we didn't talk much. Mostly I watched him play some computer game where the people looked like LEGOs. I don't get it, but it made him happy to show me."

Dani smiled. She knew which game he was talking about, and she didn't get it any more than he did. "Ah, yeah. That's his favorite game to play."

Daniel nodded. "Seems that way. So, why don't you tell me what's going on in that head of yours."

With a sigh, Dani looked down at the tea in her cup. She wished she had the power to read tea leaves. Maybe they would be able to give her an idea of what she was supposed to be doing next. "Nothing." That was false, but she wasn't sure what to say or how to start this conversation.

Her dad gave her a flat look. "Nothing. Really?" Dani shrugged before looking back down into her teacup. "I find that hard to believe, kiddo."

"I don't know what to tell you, Pop." The air went quiet between them and Dani wondered if her dad would actually believe her and change the subject to something less contentious.

"Did you know that at one point I thought about getting remarried?"

That was news enough to startle Dani. "What? When?"

Daniel shrugged. "About five years ago. There was a woman, Jane, down at the rec center."

Dani nodded slowly as she tried to recall any women named Jane. Her eyes widened when a face flashed in her mind. "Wait. You mean the woman who temporarily worked there when Rosalie was on maternity leave? Wasn't she like a decade younger than you?"

Daniel wagged his eyebrows. "I don't know why you don't think your old man still has it, but I assure you I am very much on the dating scene."

"But..." Dani trailed off as she tried to remember if she

had any suspicion. She didn't recall anything that caught her attention. She hadn't even known Daniel was dating and she was sure if she hadn't, then Ava and Vini were similarly in the dark about it. "Why didn't you then?"

"Because of you girls," he replied simply. "I knew that even if I was ready, you three weren't. Really, I wasn't ready either, so it wasn't a big enough deal for me to bring it up."

Dani reached out and cupped his hand with her own. "If you really liked her, we would have understood. We don't want you to be alone or anything, Pop."

He smiled and covered her hand with his free one. "I know that, sweetheart. It wasn't just you three that I had to think about though. I had to decide if I was in it for the right reasons. I thought long and hard and, in the end, I couldn't go through with it. I had never loved anyone as much as I loved your mother, and truthfully, I don't think I ever will."

Dani nodded. She knew her parents had had an epic love—the type that many people wrote about. She had always looked to them in awe and hoped to have a relationship that was half as successful as theirs.

"That's all to say, sometimes things don't work out and that's okay. As long as you are okay with your decisions at the end of the day." Daniel patted her hand again before sliding his away. A creak on the stairs had Dani glancing over her shoulder and her eyes widened when she saw Jordan on the step. He peered into the kitchen.

"I'm hungry."

Dani jumped up without thinking. "Let me make you something to eat, baby." She walked over to the fridge, opened it and peered inside. When small arms wrapped around her waist, she looked down. "Jordan?"

His voice was muffled against her back. "I'm sorry, Mama."

Dani felt her eyes burn and she quickly turned around, crowding him to her in a tight hug. "There's nothing to apologize for. I just want to help."

"I know," he said before sniffling. "It just feels like, first getting married and now the baby, that Dad is trying to replace me. He doesn't even really call me anymore."

Dani looked over her head at her dad, and Daniel smiled and nodded at her. She looked back down at the top of Jordan's head as she tried to think on what to say.

"Baby, sometimes people get so caught up in things that are new, that they forget to protect the things they've always had." Dani found it awfully ironic that she was saying this when she had been spending so much time cultivating her own new relationship. Were there signs that this was coming that she had missed? Surely there had been some sort of lead-up to Jacob announcing such massive changes. Maybe Dani had been spending too much time doing her own new things that she was neglecting her other responsibilities.

"But that doesn't mean they don't love you," Daniel threw out from the table. Dani smiled at him gratefully before looking back down at Jordan.

"Exactly," she said, expanding upon what he had said.

"You know your dad loves you and I know it hurts when he pays less attention to you. Those feelings are totally okay to have, and you are totally okay to tell him how you feel. I can help you if you'd like?"

Jordan wiped a hand across his face before nodding. "Yeah. Yeah, can you? I want to send him a text."

Dani knew that Jacob was probably going to blow up her phone with harsh accusations, but when Dani looked down into Jordan's hopeful face, she knew she would do anything to give him the peace of mind and closure he needed.

"I know," she said. "Why don't we go grab some lunch and then we can think about what to put in the message."

Jordan nodded. "Yeah. Okay."

Dani looked up at Daniel. "Do you want to join us, Pop?"

Daniel shook his head. "You two go enjoy your lunch. I'll hold down the fort while you're gone."

Dani nodded before looking down at Jordan. "Go grab your shoes and we'll head out. Okay?"

"Sounds good," Jordan said before hugging her quickly and scurrying from the room. Dani watched him go, her lips curled in a soft smile. She felt a little more secure; like she had finally found some stable ground. She still wasn't sure what to do about things, but she hoped getting some additional time to come up with a plan might tease something out of her.

Saturdays were always a busy day at Thomas's diner, and today was no exception. It had taken a few minutes of waiting to get a booth, but once they did, Dani felt her shoulders lighten at Jordan's pleased smile. It had been a while since they did this, and Dani knew she needed to make sure she and Jordan had more time together just the two of them. It was hard with so many things changing, but clearly this was something they both needed. Things would only continue to get busier, and they both needed to be able to pause and reset.

"What are you thinking you want to get?" Dani asked as she looked over the menu. Jordan made a considering noise before he pointed.

"I want that new hot chicken sandwich. Brody said he got it last time he came in and it was good."

Dani raised an eyebrow as she read off the description. "You know that's supposed to be spicy, right?"

Jordan made a dismissive noise. "I can handle it. I like spicy food."

"Alright, tough guy. I guess we shall see." Dani chuckled when Jordan lifted his arms in a flex, but something just beyond him caught her eye. There in the entrance was Zoey, but she wasn't alone. Dani narrowed her eyes in confusion as she tried to figure out what she was seeing. She was here with a guy Dani had never seen and they were standing way too close to be casual acquaintances. Before she could look away, the guy caught her eye and for a moment his eyes narrowed before he leaned down to whisper in Zoey's ear.

Fuck. Caught red-handed, Dani thought to herself as Zoey turned. Their gazes caught immediately, and Dani felt that familiar sense of all the air being sucked out of the room. She had forgotten how much Zoey's gaze called to her, but now she was torn between wanting to call out and wanting to run and hide. Before she could make a decision, the guy started walking toward them with Zoey hurrying after him.

Seventeen

Zoey sighed as she looked at Dani's latest message. She had been trying for two days to find some time for them to get together and introduce her to Mason. Each time, Dani had been busy, leaving Zoey to paste a fake-feeling smile on her face and explain that they wouldn't be able to get together that day. If not for showing a picture of Dani to him, she was sure Mason would have thought she was making Dani up.

"Well—"

"Let me guess," Mason said, cutting her off. "She isn't able to make it today."

Zoey winced. "Yeah," she said finally. "But we can still go ahead to the restaurant."

Mason shook his head but eventually gestured for Zoey to lead the way. Once they were in the car, she expected him to say something more but thankfully he remained quiet, giving her time to think. She was sure that the reason for Dani's continued absence had to do with Jordan. Just from the small amount of time that they had been together and from the time that she had observed Dani at the library when she was coming to get Jordan after their esports league, she knew that Dani cared very deeply for her son. It would stand to reason that being a mom was one of the most important things to her. It was one of the reasons why Zoey liked her so much. If that was the reason for their failed meetups, Zoey could extend a little grace.

Once they parked, Zoey sat for a minute in her seat. She knew that she needed to say something to break the awkwardness that she and Mason had fallen into. "She really is busy, Mason. I think maybe your visit just came at a rough time right now."

Mason sighed and looked over at Zoey. "I know you really believe that, sis, but at the same time what am I supposed to think? All I have to go on are your previous relationships, and those haven't been the best. I just want you to find someone who is deserving of your loyalty and settle down into everything that you want."

"I know," Zoey agreed. She knew that deep down that was all that her brother wanted for her. It was all she wanted for herself. She thought that she had found the beginnings of it but with each declined invitation along with Mason's pessimistic words, Zoey was starting to wonder if maybe she was reading too much into her and Dani's brief relationship. They hadn't even really discussed it to the point that she could even call it a real relationship. At least, not an exclusive one. "Let's just get some food and then we can explore Peach Blossom. I know you think I'm crazy for wanting to stay here but I think if you get out and see what the town has to offer, you might just change your mind and want to move here yourself."

Mason laughed but followed Zoey and exited the car. "I don't think small-town living is for me, but we'll see."

Thomas's diner was happening, as it usually was on a Saturday afternoon. There were a few restaurants in Peach Blossom, but Thomas's was definitely one of the most popular. Mason looked around, his eyes wide as he took everything in.

"I don't think I've ever seen an old school diner in the longest time," he said. "If the food isn't amazing here, I'm going to be really sad."

Zoey chuckled. She knew just how good the food was, so she wasn't concerned. She was looking forward to having Mason eat his words when it came to small towns not having enough to keep people interested. Sure, it wasn't Atlanta, but Peach blossom had a lot going for it.

"Oh, shit," Mason hissed out suddenly. Zoey turned to ask him what was wrong, but he leaned down. "Don't look now, but I think your pseudo girlfriend is here."

Zoey looked up at Mason, confused as to what he was talking about. His gaze slid past her and when she followed it, she was startled to realize that he was staring at Dani.

"Oh my gosh."

"I thought you said she was busy today," Mason said,

his voice growing growly, the telltale sign that he was angry. "If she's so busy that she couldn't bother to meet you, why is she sitting here in a restaurant?"

"I don't know," Zoey replied. She reached up and wrapped a hand around Mason's elbow. "Don't."

She might as well have not said anything. Before she could get a good grip on his elbow, Mason was moving toward Dani's table. Zoey hurried after him, hoping that she could get in front of Mason and keep him from causing a commotion. She didn't need her business to become fodder for the town's gossip train any more than it already was. When her and Dani's gazes connected, Zoey could see panic in Dani's expression, and she wondered about that. It wasn't until Zoey was coming to a halt beside Dani's table that she realized Jordan was sitting in the booth across from her.

"Hey, guys! Fancy meeting you here," Zoey said with forced cheerfulness, hoping to cut Mason off at the pass before he said anything untoward. Jordan looked up at her and smiled wide.

"Hey, Miss Zoey. It's cool that I get to see you here. Sorry that I wasn't at the esports club last week. I'll be back this week. I promise."

Zoey waved off his words and gave him a small smile. "It's okay, Jordan. I understand that sometimes you need to take a break. I'm glad though that we'll see you this week. I know your friends were missing you." Talking to Jordan was easy. It was turning to look at Dani that was the difficult part. Zoey could almost feel her brother vibrating at her side and she knew she needed to introduce him before things got out of hand.

"Dani, Jordan, this is my brother, Mason. He's here to visit me for the next couple days before he leaves to go overseas."

Dani stood up and held her hand out to Mason. He shook it and Zoey was relieved to see that her expression didn't change.

"Nice to meet you all," Mason said. He glanced at Jordan before fixing his eyes on Dani. "I've heard a lot about you from my sister. She said you guys have given her a warm welcome to town. I appreciate you all looking out for her while I'm gone."

Dani nodded. "Well, I know everyone in town is ecstatic to have her here. It isn't often that we get new blood to revitalize the town."

That was news to Zoey. She figured that people liked her. They never seemed to have a complaint about her when she worked with them at the library, but she never really thought about whether or not people cared if she stuck around long-term. Being in constant flux was the nature of small towns and while she knew Peach Blossom would always have a central group of families, it wouldn't be surprising if whole familial lines ended up dying out or moving out of the town and closer to a larger city, leaving holes that would never be filled.

"I have a great idea," Jordan said suddenly. "Why don't you guys sit with us?"

Zoey glanced at Dani, whose expression was one that

she couldn't distinguish. "Oh, I don't know. It looks like you and your mom are having a fun little lunch together."

"No, it's totally okay. You two are more than welcome to join us this afternoon," Dani said, surprising Zoey. "Things have been kind of hectic on our side lately and I've missed so many of our get-togethers, so this would be a great way to make up for not being able to see you for the past couple days and to get a chance to meet your brother."

"That's really sweet of you guys. We would totally love to join you."

Zoey tried to catch Mason's attention, but he either couldn't see her, or he was ignoring her as he slid into the booth. Zoey had no choice but to either slide into the booth or make up some reason for why they couldn't share. She decided to give in and slide into the seat after Mason. Dani sat back down across from her and now they were eye to eye again for the first time in a week. Zoey didn't even know what to talk about. Thankfully, Jordan was just as enthusiastic as always and took the lead in the conversation, engaging Zoey's brother with questions about being in the military.

"So, where is the coolest place you've ever visited?" Jordan asked. Dani would have told him to give Mason some time to order, but Mason seemed just as enthusiastic to talk as Jordan was.

"Thailand, hands down. The beaches were amazing, and the night markets had just about everything you could ever think of eating." When Jordan asked what a *night market* was, Mason launched into an elaborate story about wrong turns and food that sounded amazing even to Zoey's ears. She couldn't help but smile when she saw Jordan eagerly hanging on to Mason's every word. It made her chest warm that he took to her brother so easily. It shouldn't have surprised her though. Mason was great with kids, and they always seemed to be drawn to him with such little effort.

At that thought, she looked across the table in time to see Dani watching Mason and Jordan with a soft smile on her face. Zoey was slowly coming to terms with just how much she liked Dani as a person and how much she wanted this to work. Maybe Mason was right and that she fell too hard too fast, but she was all in for now. She didn't know how else to be. She didn't know how to harden her heart until the other person proved they were worthy. All she knew how to do was give and hope it was reciprocated.

"So, Dani. What do you do?" Mason asked once they had gotten their food, and the conversation had come back around. Dani paused with a fry in her hand before replying.

"I'm a nurse."

He nodded. "That's important work. Ever thought about joining the army as a medic?"

"Oh my god, Mason," Zoey cut in, shaking her head at him. Her lips twisted in a half smile, and she moved to stop him before he started his usual pitch. "Stop trying to recruit people at the lunch table."

Mason ducked his head, but his eyes were full of mirth as he looked at Dani. "Sorry. Force of habit sometimes."

Dani waved him off, not seeming the least bit offended. "It's all good. I haven't though. It's just Jordan and I, and Peach Blossom is home. I think my dad would be sad if we had to leave because I got stationed elsewhere. Plus, we have a pretty spectacular library."

Zoey felt her cheeks warm when Dani's eyes met hers. She wanted to brush the comment off, but she also didn't. It was nice to feel like someone wanted you there, especially when you wanted them too.

"The library is pretty great," Zoey replied. Jordan chimed in, making her laugh.

"And we have an esports league. I used to think libraries were just books and stuff, but it's pretty cool."

Mason smirked before glancing at Zoey. "Oh yeah? Do you think you might want to be an author then? Maybe write a few books?"

Jordan shrugged. "I don't know about that. I don't know anyone who's an author."

"Sure you do," Mason said. Zoey widened her eyes when she realized what was going on. Before she could tell him not to say anything, Mason had already blurted out her secret. "You have one right here."

Zoey swallowed hard and fought to keep the smile on her face when Dani turned curious eyes toward her. She had known that eventually she would need to come clean about her second career, but she hadn't yet figured out a way to divulge it without making things weird.

"You're an author?" Dani asked.

"Um." Zoey breathed out, giving Mason a look. The grin he gave her was unrepentant and she knew this must be another one of his little tests. She didn't know what he was trying to prove this time though. "Well...yes."

"Cool," Jordan gushed. "What do you write?"

"Nothing—"

"She writes a lot of things, but all under a pen name," Mason cut in. "I think the name was Caitlyn Martin, right?"

Silence fell for a moment and Zoey ducked her head as she looked over at Dani. She wasn't sure what she expected. Maybe admonishment or disbelief. Instead, Dani was nodding encouragingly. It took a moment before her eyes widened.

"Wait. *You're* Caitlyn Martin? Award-winning author Caitlyn Martin?"

"Guilty," Zoey said with a crooked smile.

Dani grinned widely. "Why didn't you ever say anything? I totally could have had you sign my books."

Zoey glanced at Mason's smug expression before shrugging. "I didn't want to seem like I was bragging or anything. Especially after you told me how much you liked my books. It seemed weird to then mention I was the author."

Dani nodded. "I can see that. But, brag as much as you want. There's no shame in shouting out your accomplishments, and having a bestselling book is definitely an accomplishment."

Mason threw an arm around Zoey's shoulders. "Isn't my baby sister the coolest?"

"She is pretty great," Dani said, her voice going soft as she gazed at Zoey. The look in her eyes was enough to have Zoey's cheeks heating up and something clenching in her chest. "Can I ask you something?"

Zoey shrugged off Mason's hold and leaned forward. "Of course. You can ask me anything." Maybe it was a bit much, but Zoey couldn't help it.

Dani's serious expression finally broke when she smirked. "Can you tell me when the sequel to your latest book is coming out? I need to read it as soon as possible."

Zoey blinked for a moment before beside her, Mason let out a loud bark of laughter. Dani sat back as if satisfied with herself. When bubbles of laughter rose in her chest, Zoey didn't fight against them, instead giving them voice as the afternoon passed them pleasantly by.

Eighteen

"I like her."

Zoey paused where she was reaching into the fridge to turn and look at Mason. He was putting clothes in his suitcase and not looking at her, but she knew he could tell she was looking at him.

"You like who?"

He looked up with a bland expression. "Your sugar mommy."

It was a good thing she wasn't drinking anything, otherwise it might have ended up everywhere. She pulled out the bottle of juice she was reaching for and straightened up. "I don't have a sugar... You are so weird."

He grinned before shrugging. "It is what it is. But anyway, I retract my earlier statements. I like her and having seen you two interact, I feel good about letting you date her."

"You don't *let* me do anything, asshole." She threw a

dish towel at him, feeling satisfied when it tagged Mason on the side of the head. He threw it off and scowled at her, looking like a little kid. "I wasn't basing my choice off of what you said."

"So, you wouldn't have considered my thoughts at all?"

She wanted to say no, but Zoey truly did value Mason's opinions. He wasn't always right about things, but he was more objective when it came to this case. If he had left the lunch and immediately told Zoey to get the hell away from Dani, she might have had to seriously consider it. "I would have considered them, but in the end, the decision is mine alone."

"Of course," he agreed easily. "You're a grown-ass woman now. All I can do is provide my brotherly advice and hope you take it."

Zoey poured them both some juice before walking over and handing Mason his glass. "Okay, and what brotherly advice do you have for me now?" She knew even with Mason saying that he liked Dani that he probably had more comments and concerns to convey.

Mason took the glass before taking a sip. He smacked his lips exaggeratedly before speaking. "My only advice to you is to take it slow and to really think about whether or not this relationship serves not only you but also Dani. Dating as a single parent is tough—I should know that. It means that she is going to have to consider Jordan before anything else, including herself. Including you."

"I know that," Zoey said. She truly did know that. She had seen the sacrifices that Mason had made when raising her. She knew that part of the reason why he was still single even after all these years was because he got used to it. He was enjoying the freedom of not having responsibilities and he deserved to, after partially putting his life on hold to raise her. Despite what Mason said though, Zoey knew that he still considered her as much as he could when making decisions about his own future. They had had many arguments with her telling him to put himself first when it came to what he decided to do next. His upcoming move meant that maybe he was finally taking what she said seriously.

"You say that, sis, but I don't think you really understand what that means," he said gently. Zoey narrowed her eyes and opened her mouth to speak, but Mason put a hand on her arm, halting her words. "No, listen to what I have to say first. I don't mean that you would do something to mess things up on purpose. But, things are even more complicated for the two of you because you have already met Jordan and he already seems fond of you."

"He's an amazing kid," Zoey threw out.

"Absolutely he is. And I can't blame him for liking you. You're my sister, so I know how amazing you are. But that also makes it more difficult if things don't work out between you and Dani."

"Do you ever regret it?" Zoey asked, looking down at her cup. "Choosing to take me in, I mean. Do you ever regret doing that?"

"Never," Mason said, his voice fiercer than she had ever heard it.

"But, you were so young," she continued. There hadn't been many options back then. Zoey had gone to stay with their paternal aunt and her husband for a few months, and they had been very nice. But they had three kids of their own and not enough time or space. Zoey hadn't been mistreated, but she had almost immediately faded into the background of the life they had already established. She still kept in contact with them, but she hadn't been sad when Mason had arrived and announced he was going to be taking her with him when he left.

Mason leaned against her, his larger shoulder pushing her against the couch. Zoey couldn't help but laugh and push against him. He flopped over her like he had always done when they were kids.

"So were you," he said as he pushed back up, letting Zoey go. "We were both young, but we had each other. I wasn't about to be separated from you. Not if I could help it."

Zoey smiled. "I feel the same, really. I just don't like the idea that you never got to have your wild streak because of me."

Mason laughed, throwing his head back before looking at her with familiar crinkled eyes. "That you thought I didn't have time to have fun means I did a great job. I had plenty of time when I needed it. Please believe that, and don't feel guilty. If anything, you kept me from making some really idiotic decisions that would have made both of our lives harder."

Zoey nodded. She didn't say anything, despite wanting to push back immediately. Instead, she let his words wash over her. Zoey knew that no one went into a relationship expecting to break up. But sometimes—hell, often—if she was being honest, things happened. She too had some concerns about the fact that she was already involved in Jordan's life. She knew herself and she knew that if she and Dani broke up, she wouldn't treat him any differently. But it was still something that she had to really think about.

She didn't doubt that Dani was having similar conversations with her family and friends, and she knew that at some point if they both decided that they wanted to continue this relationship and maybe move it to the next level, they needed to have this conversation together.

"So, like I said," Mason continued, grabbing her attention again. "I like Dani. I like the fact that there's another person telling you to celebrate yourself. And as much as it pains me as your brother to admit, I like that she couldn't take her eyes off of you while we were eating."

Zoey nearly spit her juice out and covered her mouth with her hand as she looked at Mason. She hadn't noticed Dani doing anything unusual or staring at her any longer than she normally did. Was there something that she was missing?

"What do you mean?"

Mason gave her a look. "You really didn't see how she was looking at you? Zoey, come on."

Zoey pushed his shoulder. "Shut up. Make sure you have your passport so we can go." She stood up from the couch and walked away to keep from showing just how flustered Mason's last comments had made her. She had a lot to think about.

Zoey had a little pep in her step today as she walked into the library for her shift. Mondays were normally rough, but she couldn't find it in herself to be down today. Her weekend had been too damn good, and she was still riding the high of it into a new workday. She had just reached the staff room when her cell rang, and Zoey quickly moved to answer it.

"Hello?"

"Should you be on your phone in the library, Ms. Big Name Author?"

Zoey couldn't help the smile that lit up her face when she heard Dani's voice over the line. They hadn't seen each other yesterday because Zoey had gone up to Atlanta to take Mason to the airport so he could catch his flight out.

"'Ms. Big Name Author'? Is that what we're going with these days?"

Dani's soft chuckle had Zoey clutching at her cell. That sound did things for her, and she wanted to wrap it around her and pull it out whenever she needed a fix.

"Am I wrong?"

"No," Zoey admitted. She still felt weird about saying that, but Mason had been on to her for years about downplaying her achievements. With both of them tag-teaming her, Zoey figured she should probably start listening and tooting her own horn a little. "Why are you up so early? I thought you were off today?"

"I am," Dani replied. "But I wanted to catch you before your shift started and make sure you were okay. I know you had to take Mason to the airport last night. It was tough enough for me to watch Vini drive away, and I knew she would be back in like two weeks. I can't imagine having to say goodbye to your brother for months, if not years, at a time."

Zoey felt warmed by the thought of Dani caring about her. "I think I'm used to it at this point. But thank you for checking on me."

"Of course," Dani said as if it were the most normal thing in the world and not something that rearranged Zoey's feelings from the inside out. How was she supposed to take things slow in the face of Dani's kindness? "I've got to head out, but Jordan will be in later for the esports league. He didn't want to miss another week."

"Great. I'll look out for him. I know the other boys will be happy he's back." They said their goodbyes and Zoey stood staring at the phone before her alarm went off and she headed back out to the main area to get started on the day's responsibilities.

The morning went by quickly. It was fairly quiet for a Monday morning, but Zoey appreciated having the time to catalog some of the books she'd missed last week. She still didn't know what was going on with the board proposal, but Tiffany had assured her that Zoey staying was what everyone wanted. There had been buzz over the past couple weeks about some car manufacturing plant being built not too far outside of town that would possibly have trickle effects on Peach Blossom's population. Zoey knew that more opportunity meant more chances for the town to stabilize or even grow. She liked this place, and she hoped things went through to keep it around.

By the time she came up from her duties, she realized it was time to get the computer room set up for the league. She had just finished getting the desktops running when she heard the boys' voices.

"Hi, Ms. Zoey."

She turned with a wide smile, waving them in. "Hey, Henry. Come on in and get started, boys. I have everything set up for you."

They rushed in, muted laughter and jokes filling the space with new energy. It invigorated Zoey, giving her a slight boost that would hopefully carry her through the next couple hours before the end of her workday. She went to her usual desk where she stayed to monitor them for a bit. When Jordan walked in, she expected him to be as upbeat as his friends, so she was surprised when he gave her a half-hearted wave before slinking over to his usual computer. She saw one of the other boys give him a quick side hug before they started playing.

"I wonder what that was all about," she mumbled to herself. She resolved to pay close attention to see if something was going on between the boys.

The next couple hours, Zoey went back and forth between the computer room and the circulation desk and each time, she glanced over at Jordan. He had perked up somewhat, but he still wasn't his usual self. She tried to remember if he or Dani had mentioned anything at the diner Saturday. She had noticed he was a little quiet when they first sat down, but once he and Mason started talking, Jordan was his usual outgoing self. Now, there was very little sign of the outgoing Jordan from before. Zoey made a note to talk to him and hoped she wasn't overstepping. It wasn't anything she wouldn't do for one of the other kids if she saw they were acting the same, but it did have her considering every angle, given her new relationship with Dani.

When the boys were cleaning up and about to go, Zoey called out to Jordan, asking for a moment before he left. Jordan waved bye to the other boys before walking up to her.

"Jordan? Is everything okay?"

He frowned. "What do you mean?"

She paused for a moment, considering her words very carefully. "I mean, you don't seem like your usual happy self. I just wanted to check in to see if there was anything going on or if you needed anything when it came to the team. Is it too much pressure? I know we have our first league matchup coming soon so that can be stressful."

Jordan shrugged before looking down at the ground. Zoey wasn't sure what to do with that, but she didn't feel comfortable pushing him if he didn't want to talk. She was about to move away and say goodbye when he finally looked up. His expression changed to one of determination. "My dad is getting married again."

Zoey widened her eyes. That was definitely new information to her. Dani rarely talked about her ex-husband, and other than a couple questions thrown out here and there, Zoey had never really asked. She had a general idea of what had gone down with Dani's previous relationship and that was good enough for her.

"I see. How does that make you feel?"

Jordan lifted his shoulders again before looking away. "It's okay, I guess. But..." He trailed off. He looked so uncomfortable, and Zoey almost hated to ask. But it seemed like he wanted to talk about it, and Zoey wanted to be here for him.

"But what?"

He glanced at her before continuing. "He's going to have a baby with his girlfriend. He even said he's going to name it after him instead of a different name like me."

Damn. Zoey could see how that might be jarring for the kid, and she immediately felt bad for him. She couldn't imagine how it felt that not only was your dad having a baby, but he was also doing something for the baby he didn't do for you. Some kids wouldn't care, sure, but it seemed like it mattered to Jordan a lot.

"Have you talked to your dad about it?"

Jordan shifted his backpack on his shoulder. "I tried to, but he told me I should just be happy for him. He's replacing my mom and me, but I'm supposed to be happy. It's so stupid." Zoey could hear the frustration clear in his voice and she wished she had something she could say that would make everything better for him. She didn't have much experience when it came to parental dynamics, especially when parents were split up and coparenting. *This must have been why Dani was so hit-or-miss last week.* It made sense. If she were trying to find the words for helping Jordan, she probably didn't have time to worry about anyone else. It was exactly as Mason had said, but Zoey wasn't upset about having been relegated to the background. She was upset that she couldn't do more for Jordan. Clearly, he was struggling with what were about to be new experiences and dynamics. Middle school was a tough time, even before adding in complicated family dynamics. A knock on the door pulled her from her introspection and she called out for the person to come in.

"I'm here to pick up Jordan."

"Grandpa!" Jordan's excitement brought a little comfort to Zoey, and she called out her own goodbyes when he and his grandfather left. As Zoey walked around, double-checking things were clean and ready for the next group, she resolved to figure out a way to talk to Dani. She wasn't sure there was anything tangible she could do, but the least she could offer was a friendly ear.

Nineteen

Dani told herself she wasn't gearing up for a fight. Sure, she had called her ex-husband and told him that he needed to physically come inside to pick Jordan up for his weekend, but she wasn't planning on jumping him or anything. They just needed to have a conversation and talk some things out.

All week, Jordan had been almost a shell of his normal boisterous self. He had done his homework like normal. He went to his esports club and talked with his friends. Dani had even had to remind him not to get too loud when he was in his room playing games online. But still, there were times when maybe he thought no one was paying attention that Dani would see his happy expression fall, leaving his face devoid of anything. She knew instinctively that he was still trying to come to terms with the changes his dad had foisted on him. The worst part was that Dani was still not sure how to help.

She and Jacob didn't often discuss their private lives. She had met his fiancée years ago and she didn't have anything against the woman. She was nice enough and as long as Jordan never had any complaints, Dani was happy to keep things pushing. Now though, something needed to happen. A knock on her bedroom door startled her from her thoughts and Dani looked up in time to see Daniel in the doorway. His expression was solemn as he looked at her.

"Jacob is coming up the drive."

She nodded. "Thanks, Pop. Keep Jordan up in his room and occupied for a bit, alright? He doesn't need to be part of this conversation just yet."

"I agree. But you let me know if I need to come down."

Dani smiled. She knew her dad had her back, as would Ava if she let her. Dani had purposely told Ava to leave the house after divulging the news of Jacob's impending nuptials. Dani had had to keep her from marching over to Jacob's and telling him about himself. Ava might not have kids of her own, but she always went to bat for Jordan. It made Dani feel good to know that not only she, but Jordan had a support system here that would take care of him no matter what.

She walked into the hallway and knocked on Jordan's door. She waited for him to call out before she cracked it open and stuck her head in. "Your dad is here. I'm going to talk with him a bit and then Grandpa Daniel will let you know to come down, okay?"

Jordan gave her a distracted nod. His gaze was still

trained on the computer screen. "Alright, Mom. Try not to get too heated."

Dani snorted. "Come on. It's me we're talking about. If it were your aunt Ava though…" She trailed off, delighting in the way Jordan chuckled at her words. The whole family was in agreement that Ava was the winner when it came to anger issues, with Daniel coming in at a close second. "I love you, kiddo."

Jordan glanced at her then with a lopsided smile. "I know, Mom."

Dani rolled her eyes before ducking back out of the room and closing the door. She didn't doubt that Jordan would try his best to sneak a listen, but Daniel was upstairs and would keep the worst of Jordan's curiosity at bay. When Dani got downstairs, she had to take a deep breath before opening the front door. Jacob looked the same as always. At one point in time, Dani had thought he was the most attractive boy she'd ever met. That was before she had ever left Peach Blossom. Objectively, he was still good-looking, but he did nothing for her anymore.

"Hey," Jacob said glancing around. "Where's Jordan? Isn't he ready to go?"

"He is, but I had mentioned needing to talk to you, remember?"

Jacob sighed and put his hands on his hips. "Dani, I have a lot to get done today. I don't have time for this."

She folded her arms, giving him a heated look. "This is about our son, so I suggest you make time." Her voice had gone hard, and she knew she struck her mark when

Jacob's eyes widened. "Come inside and sit down. I have things to do as well, so I'm not trying to take up all of your or my time."

Dani moved back, allowing Jacob to walk into the house. She closed the door behind them and glanced at the stairs, hoping that Jordan had his headphones on and was engaged in a game rather than paying attention to what was going on downstairs. She led Jacob over to the couch, sat down and gestured for him to do the same. It was the first time he had been inside the home in a long time. Jacob glanced at the stairs before sighing again and sitting on the edge of the couch. It was strange to see him sitting again on the couch after years of absence. It was uncomfortable in a way that Dani wasn't expecting.

"Okay, you have me here. Now, let's talk about whatever it is you think is the issue quickly so I can get going. What's going on?"

Dani was doing her best not to let her attitude get in the way of the conversation they needed to have, but it was hard. She was normally a chill person, but for some reason, Jacob was one of the people who just always got under her skin. This was part of the reason why they hadn't been able to work out all those years ago. It had been like trying to combine oil and water. All it did was make a huge mess. Even on a good day, trying to have a hard conversation with Jacob was worse than trying to pull teeth that weren't ready to be removed.

"Jordan let me know that you are getting married next year."

Jacob nodded quickly. "Shit, yeah, I am. Sorry that I didn't let you know first but we're still at the beginning of planning and nothing's even close to being finalized yet. We haven't even picked a date."

Dani waved off his words. "That's fine. I'm happy for you both. It just would have been good to get a little heads-up for Jordan's sake." She was trying to keep the conversation focused on their son and not on how much she wanted to throttle Jacob. She doubted that he had forgotten to tell her about the proposal and wedding. It was far more likely that he just didn't want to and hoped that everything would happen before she found out. "He's been a little upset lately, especially after that night."

Jacob rolled his eyes before shaking his head. "There was nothing wrong with him sitting on the front porch waiting for you. I told him to keep his behind in the house, but he insisted that he was grown," he said, trying to justify it. "If I had known that you were going to freak out about it so much, I would have let you know ahead of time so you could prepare yourself instead of blowing up my phone with text messages after the fact."

"I don't think it was out of line for me to suggest that letting our eleven-year-old son sit outside in the dark by himself was a bad idea," she countered. "We might not be concerned with people coming by to snatch him up, but never mind the fact that we got coyotes prowling all over the place. Didn't anything like that ever cross your mind?"

"Of course it didn't cross my mind because it wasn't

very likely," Jacob said, frustration coloring his voice. "Nothing happened but some hurt feelings and maybe a mosquito bite or two, and he learned a valuable lesson about picking and choosing your battles. He called you to pick him up and you came. There's no reason to draw this out unnecessarily."

Dani begged to differ, but it was clear that Jacob was not going to see reason. He was so sure that everything he had done was correct that even if Jordan had been crying his eyes out, Dani doubted he would have apologized or even said that he did anything wrong. "And what about naming your new baby after yourself? Did you not stop to think that maybe Jordan would feel some type of way once he found out?"

"I don't think what we name our future baby is any of yours or Jordan's concern. Besides, it was your fault I didn't name him after me in the first damn place," he replied. He stood up from the couch. "Is this seriously what you brought me in here to talk about? Are you really so petty that you would want to ruin my happiness just because Jordan isn't getting his way for once?"

Dani looked up at him in disgust. "You really think that Jordan has been upset for the past week simply because he isn't getting his way? Is that truly something that just came out of your mouth right now?"

"I don't know what else it could be. It's not like I'm the only one who has moved on. Word on the street is that you're all over the town with someone who might not even be here in a year," he accused. "Which do you think is going to cause more lasting damage when it comes to Jordan? Him seeing me in a long-term, healthy relationship, or you hopping from one person to the next depending on who shows you attention?"

Dani's stomach dropped at Jacob's words. She knew that really, he was just trying to get a rise out of her and hurt her as a way to defend his own actions. Still, she couldn't deny that there was a thread of truth there. She was seemingly moving on with someone who was already in Jordan's life. They hadn't gotten to the point where they were really discussing exclusivity or their plans for the future, but Dani knew that if things went bad between her and Zoe it could affect Jordan in a very real way. But what was Jacob talking about Zoe potentially not being here in a year? Did he know something she didn't?

"I don't know what you're talking about when it comes to time frames and why that has any relevance to what Jordan is going through right now," she said, trying to keep the subject focused on the here and now. "I haven't said anything to Jordan about me dating because none of it has gotten serious to the point that he needs to concern himself with it. I've already said if anything ever gets to that point then I would have a conversation with you."

"You didn't think it was already serious enough, considering the fact that she is sponsoring one of the clubs that our son is in?"

"No, because I can still walk away, and Jordan would be none the wiser. Rumors start every day in this town.

It doesn't mean that they're all correct. But you have confirmed something that affects him and all I'm asking is that you take the time to truly think about things and talk to your son the way he deserves."

"No, what I deserve is to not be ambushed because you're jealous that I've moved on and you haven't." Jacob's words and his continued stubbornness had Dani jumping up from the couch.

"What the hell do I have to be jealous about, Jacob? I'm not the one who cheated and broke up our family."

"Well, clearly it wouldn't have worked out anyway because you don't even date men anymore." How the conversation had spiraled so heavily out of control Dani wasn't even sure. "How do you think Jordan is going to feel, considering he has his own crush on his favorite librarian?"

Dani froze. This was news to her. She knew that Jordan was fond of Zoey, but he had never said anything about potentially having a crush on her. It didn't matter of course in the grand scheme of things, but it was just one more thing that Dani now had to worry about that she hadn't planned for.

"You spend all this time judging me and yet you're the one making decisions without considering the long-term effects on the people around you." Dani knew Jacob was talking shit, but like always he was able to pinpoint some of her greatest insecurities and weaponize them, leaving her feeling off kilter and unsure of her next move. Footsteps on the stairs had Dani glancing over her shoulder just in time to see Jordan come tumbling down the steps. His lips were turned down in a scowl and his dark brown eyes were trained on Jacob.

"Dad, why would you tell Mom that? I told you that stuff in secret," Jordan said, his voice loud and laced with anger.

"Your mom and I were just having a conversation," Jacob said. "Go get your stuff so we can get out of here."

Jordan shook his head. "I'm not going."

Dani's eyes widened and she took a step toward Jordan. She put on her calmest voice and hoped that she could defuse the situation before it spiraled even more out of control. "Jordan, it's fine, sweetheart. It's time for you to go with your dad and I'll see you on Monday."

He turned to look at Dani and she froze again. Never had she seen Jordan so angry before. "No, I said I'm not going." Before Dani could reach out, Jordan turned and ran back up the stairs. His footsteps rang out against the hardwood until they were followed by the slam of his bedroom door. For a moment she wasn't sure what to do. Even as a toddler, Jordan had been fairly easygoing and kept his tantrums at a minimum. This moodiness was brand-new behavior.

"I don't need this shit," Jacob hissed. Dani turned to see him swipe a hand over his face. His lips were turned down in a scowl just like the one she had seen on Jordan's face. "I have things to do, so you let me know if Jordan is ready to act like he has some sense."

"What are you talking about?" Dani asked in confusion. "Are you seriously just going to leave and not go up and say anything to him?"

"He wants to act all big and bad, yelling at people like he's grown. Fine. He can have these grown consequences."

Dani shook her head in disbelief. Now she was really and truly angry. She was angry at Jacob for acting like this toward their son. And she was angry at herself for ever thinking that he would be a good father to begin with.

"You are truly unbelievable," she said quietly. "Go. I'll take care of Jordan, just like I always do. I hope you're a better father to this new baby than you have been. I truly do."

She could tell that something about her words had resonated with him. Jacob opened and closed his mouth a few times, but no words came. He glanced at the stairs one more time before making a hurt-sounding noise and turning to exit the living room. Dani heard the front door open and slam closed a few moments later. She had hoped that having a conversation would help solve things, but now Dani was worried that things were worse than ever.

Twenty

Work had been uneventful, which was good considering the fact that Dani was still reeling from the events of the weekend. Jacob never came back for Jordan, and Jordan never asked to go to his house either. Instead, Jordan had spent most of the time holed up in his room, only coming out when Dani had yelled up the stairs that dinner was ready. Dinner that night had been a quiet affair. Dani hadn't known what to say and even when Daniel tried to get some sort of conversation going, Jordan had only responded with one-word answers. As soon as the last of the food had been consumed, Jordan had made a quick escape back to his room. Dani had checked on him a couple of times before letting him know it was time for bed. The one time she tried to broach the subject of his dad, Jordan had given her a look so somber that she almost apologized before changing the subject.

By the time Sunday rolled around, anger had overtaken

Dani's sadness, and she refused to let Jordan hide away in his room any longer. She had carted him down the road to the nearest farm to do a little strawberry picking. It was a bit early in the season, but she had fond memories of going with her sisters when they were younger. It was also one of the places their parents would take them when it was time to have family discussions. There was something rhythmic and calming about picking that helped settle them enough to form the right words. Dani hadn't taken Jordan there in a while, but she figured now was as good a time as any to continue the tradition.

It had taken a little while to get him to open up, but once they had filled up half of their basket Jordan had finally started giving more than one-word answers to even the most basic of questions. Dani hadn't wanted to break the peace they had fallen into by going too deep into things, but she needed to reiterate to Jordan that no matter what, she was here for him. The car ride back home seemed as perfect a time as any.

"So, what did you think? Should we come back before the picking season ends?"

Jordan nodded. "Yeah. We should bring Grandpa next time. He could hold more strawberries." Dani snorted. She wasn't opposed to bring someone else in to do the heavy lifting. "Or…" Jordan's voice trailed off.

Dani glanced over at him. "'Or'? Is there someone else you were thinking of inviting?"

"Maybe… Ms. Zoey?"

Dani's heart thumped in her chest. She tightened her

hold on the steering wheel before taking a deep breath in. "Oh? Why is that?"

"Because I maybe...like her." Jordan clenched his fists before crossing his arms over his chest. "I know it's a stupid crush, but she's cool. She lets me talk to her about video games and she actually knows the ones I talk about."

"Hey," Dani said, interrupting him. She reached out and patted his thigh. "It's okay. Zoey is pretty cool. I'm sure she would enjoy strawberry picking too."

"You think?" The hesitancy in his voice was nearly heartbreaking and Dani reassured him.

"Absolutely," she said confidently. "Besides, anyone who doesn't like strawberry picking is a noob and deeply uncool." She grinned at him, feeling nothing but pride when he cringed.

"Mom, nobody says that anymore."

The rest of the car ride was still quiet, but the tension that had existed previously had melted away.

Monday was better, with Jordan slowly going back to his normal happy self and Dani felt better about the direction everything was going in. She worked into the evening, so she wasn't there when Daniel picked Jordan up from his esports league at the library, which meant she wasn't able to see or talk to Zoey in person. They had been texting though, leading up to tonight's book club. For all of five minutes, Dani thought about skipping it, given all of the recent turmoil that had been going on in the house but when she talked to Jordan and Daniel, both of them insisted that she get out of the house and go.

You don't get out very often at all, Mom. Go and have fun. Grandpa and I are going to hang out so I can teach him how to play my favorite video game.

Dani had checked with her dad just to make sure he really was okay with staying in with Jordan for the night and once she confirmed it, they both practically pushed her out the door. She wasn't sure whether to feel some type of way about them trying to get rid of her. Then again, the two of them did enjoy doing their grandpa-grandson bonding activities. Dani was never really sure what they did during that time, but as long as nobody was bleeding when she got home it was none of her business.

When Dani walked into book club, she felt a familiar sense of calm wash over her. As much as she wanted to be there for Jordan, there seemed to be no outward lasting effects from the argument she and Jacob had had over this past weekend. She also knew that downtime was just as important for her as it was for them. She knew it was going to be a long uphill battle leading up to Jacob's wedding, and she was already dreading what she knew would be additional arguments.

"Dani. So good to see you," Tiffany said. She handed Dani a cup before herding her into Zoey's apartment.

Dani looked down into the cup, confused. "What is this?"

Tiffany's smile was wide. "I decided to make some sangrias, but don't worry—they're not that strong and there's plenty of water." Dani took a sip, enjoying the bold fruity flavors that danced on her tongue. When she walked into the living room, she waved at the familiar faces, exchanging hellos as people talked softly catching up on all the events that had occurred over the past week. When Dani saw Zoey, she couldn't help but smile. It hadn't been that long since they last saw each other, and yet she found herself greedy for a glimpse of that familiar yellow cardigan and those curls that she knew were pleasantly soft to the touch. There were still things that she needed to talk to Zoey about, and she had some book-related questions that didn't concern book club.

When Zoey caught sight of her, her smile was exquisite, and she ducked her head as if bashful. She could be the cutest thing that Dani had ever seen and yet Dani still remembered the hunger with which their lips met. Had it really only been a couple weeks since their first kiss? They had been taking things slowly, but Dani was hungry for more.

Zoey slid a tray on the coffee table before addressing the group. "Okay, everyone please feel free to eat and drink as much as you want as always, but let's get into our book for this upcoming month."

Dani had bought the book already. It was one that she was superexcited about, and it had been tough not to read too far ahead of where they were supposed to for tonight's discussion. Over the next hour, Dani let herself fall into the world between the pages. It was nice to be able to pretend that she was someone else. She had thought that this book would be one of her favorites, and she was right. The writing had let her jump right into the words and Dani was not too proud to admit that she had gone back and bought every book in the author's backlist. She figured it was a belated gift to herself for putting up with people's shenanigans day in and day out. It might have blown her book budget for the next couple months, but she couldn't find it in herself to be upset about that.

"What do you think, Dani?" Tiffany asked, catching Dani's attention. "From what we've read so far, are you getting the feeling that this is going to be a plot-driven or character-driven book?"

Dani thought on it for a moment, tapping her chin with her finger. "This is giving character driven for me. I mean, the setting is pulling me in as well. It's really giving early nineties nostalgia but beyond that, I really feel it's the characters that are leading the way for this book so far." She looked around and saw some of the others nodding in agreement.

"I have to agree with you there," Zoey said. Dani couldn't help but watch as her long fingers brushed over the pages of the book in her hands. Dani's mouth went dry imagining how those fingers would feel against her skin. It was a terrible time to be thinking of things that were very much not book related, but she and Zoe had been casually seeing each other for weeks and they had yet to go beyond kissing and a little grinding action. It wasn't the slowest that she'd ever gone with someone she was seeing, but it definitely was leaving Dani frustrated and damn near gagging for more.

The group took a break after about an hour of discussion and Dani followed Zoey into the adjacent kitchen. Her living, dining and kitchen space was all open but there were columns that gave an illusion of privacy. Dani had a few questions she wanted to ask Zoey, and she didn't want to particularly do it with a live audience. When Zoey noticed that Dani had followed her to the kitchen, she turned with a smile.

"Hey, is there anything that I can get for you while we're in here?"

Dani shook her head. "No, I'm good. I did have a couple questions for you though, if you have the time?"

Zoe nodded. "Of course, I have time. What's going on? Is everything okay?"

Dani glanced over her shoulder before looking back at Zoey. She was pretty sure nobody was paying any attention to them, but she would do her best to keep it vague just in case. "I don't know if you heard, but Jordan's dad is getting married."

Zoey nodded. "Jordan did mention something about that at the esports club last week."

That surprised Dani. She had thought that Jordan wasn't really opening up to anyone. She wasn't sure how she felt about the fact that Jordan had opened up to Zoey already before he really talked about it with her. On one hand, Dani was happy that Jordan felt comfortable enough with Zoey to go to her for questions or if he had concerns. On the other hand, she wasn't sure if that was muddying the waters a little too much a little too soon. Jacob's words still echoed in her memory, and she hoped that getting involved with someone who was already entrenched in her kid's life was not going to be an issue.

"How is he handling the news?"

"Well, he isn't taking it the best. I don't think it helps that his dad and his dad's fiancée are also expecting a new baby. It's been a lot for him to take in," Dani said. Zoey's eyes were wide and her lips were slightly parted. It was simultaneously hilarious and adorable to see her so lost for words.

"Well, yeah, I can imagine that that would be a lot for him to take in all at once," Zoey replied. "Is he okay with everything?"

"I mean, he's as good as he's going to be while he processes it, but I was hoping that you might have some book recommendations that I could buy or check out that might help facilitate a conversation that I know we need to have."

Zoey nodded. "Yeah, I definitely know of a couple books that might be helpful to at least get the conversation going. I could text you over the list of them tomorrow once I get to work, if that works for you?"

Dani agreed, feeling better about things now that she had the beginnings of a plan. She knew coming to Zoey would be a good idea, if only to get some resources to help Dani formulate talking points that she could use in a conversation with Jordan. She didn't think she would be able to appeal to any sort of logic when it came to Jacob, and she wasn't even going to waste her energy to try.

"That works perfectly," Dani replied with a grateful smile. "I don't know what I would do without your help. Thanks so much, Zoey."

Zoey shrugged. "Of course. I might have a couple books here in the house that you might find helpful if you want to stay after book club. That way, you can take them home and go through them and see if anything is helpful before I text you out the second list tomorrow."

Dani nodded in agreement just as everyone else in the living room called them back. Zoey gave her a small smile but before she walked by, she also brushed her lips against Dani's cheek. It was a simple little touch and yet it meant just about everything to Dani in that moment. It was a comfort and one that she hadn't even realized she needed until then. Maybe that made her weak; Dani didn't know. All she knew was that she felt a newfound sense of strength as she walked back into the living room and prepared to discuss books with people who were quickly becoming friends. When it was time to pack up and leave to head home after another successful book club, Dani took the plates and cups into the kitchen, intent on helping out.

"You didn't need to do that," Zoey said as she walked into the kitchen. Dani glanced at her from over her shoulder. "I could have gotten it in the morning."

"You've been such a big help that the least I can do is a couple of dishes. It's really not that big a deal. You should see how many I have to do when I'm at home," Dani joked. She was expecting Zoey to laugh but she wasn't expecting to feel the heat of her against her back or to find herself shivering as a pair of arms snaked around her waist. Dani leaned back into the comforting embrace. It was nice to just be for a moment. With everything that was going on, Dani didn't often get moments like this. Before she could second-guess herself, she turned in Zoey's embrace and wrapped her own arms around her waist.

"Dani?" Zoey asked softly.

She didn't answer, instead fitting her face in the space between Zoey's chin and shoulder. "Can we just stay like this for a moment?" She braced herself for the questions she wasn't ready for. Her surprise when Zoey nodded felt a lot like relief.

"Of course. Take all the time you need."

Twenty-One

The back porch was bathed in a soft glow as the sun set beyond the tree line. Dani shivered slightly as she pulled her sweater more tightly around her shoulders. The afternoon was calm as she breathed deeply, letting her thoughts drift along. Work had been relatively low-key today, which was a blessing and a curse. A blessing because it gave her time to think on other things as she made her rounds. A curse…for the same damn reason. Dani's thoughts were a tangled mess that she was still trying to make sense of. Every time she thought she had a hold on things, something else popped up, sending her careening again as her thoughts raced to the bottom.

"Here you are," Ava said, popping up behind her. Dani turned as she walked through the doorway. "What are you doing out here? I thought you were going to hang out with Zoey tonight."

Dani nodded. "I am. She has a phone call with her agent though, so we're pushing things back an hour."

"Ah. It's kind of cool that you know someone who's an author, and your favorite one at that." She walked around Dani before dropping down onto the bench beside her. "Think she would be cool with me asking her to come speak to my class about writing and stuff?"

Dani shrugged. "You should ask her, but I don't think she would mind. She's talked before about starting a youth book club to get more kids interested in reading and writing."

"That's good to know. I might ask her questions just about being an author in general."

"Are you still thinking about writing that book?" Dani asked. It was nice to be able to talk about anything but her own problems. "What was the book about again?"

Ava snorted softly. "Which one?" When Dani glanced at her, she grinned. "I have a lot of book ideas, but I'm still not sure which one I want to lead with. It's nerve-racking to put yourself out there when there's no guarantee that it'll be well received."

Man, wasn't that the truth. Dani could understand that on multiple levels. Right now, she was also wondering if she had been putting herself out there a little too much as of late. As much as she knew Jacob was full of shit sometimes, his words still occasionally found their mark with her and now she was left wondering if maybe she was too close to things to see if she'd miscalculated something along the way.

"Why are you so quiet today?"

Dani glanced at her. "Aren't you usually the one telling me to shut up?"

"I mean, yeah, but not really. I don't want you to actually be quiet," Ava said. She jostled Dani's shoulder with her own. "What's going on? Is it about Jordan?"

Dani didn't want to talk about it, but maybe that was her whole problem. She couldn't keep everything bound up inside her head without going a little crazy with only her own thoughts for comfort.

"Sort of," she conceded. It took her a moment to find her words. "Do you think I rushed into dating too soon?"

Ava raised an eyebrow. "Rushed? You didn't date for like two years and even after you started, I think you went out like once or twice a year. You didn't do it enough if you ask me."

"Yeah, but what about Jordan?" Dani asked. "I didn't want to make him uncomfortable."

"And you haven't. At least not that he's told any of us, and you know Dad would be the first person to sit us down if his grandson wasn't happy about something. He loves Jordan more than us."

Dani chuckled along with Ava at the long-running family joke. She knew their father didn't love one of them more than the other, but he absolutely favored Jordan against the rest of them simply by virtue of him being the only grandchild.

"True," Dani admitted. "But—"

"Did Jacob say something to you?" Ava cut in. She narrowed her eyes when Dani opened and closed her mouth a few times without saying anything. "I swear that ass-hole is looking for trouble. What did he say this time?"

She shook her head. "Nothing that I can't handle." It was true. Dani could handle whatever was thrown at her. Hell, she didn't have a choice. She couldn't fall apart just because someone said something mean to her. "I just... Do you find it weird that I haven't had a steady relation-ship since the divorce?"

Ava shrugged. "Not particularly. Pop never did either after...you know."

"But that's different," Dani insisted.

"Is it?"

Dani thought about it. "I mean, maybe."

Ava sat back and crossed her arms as they both looked out over the backyard as the sun slowly dipped farther be-hind the trees. The air was cooler now than it had been a few minutes ago and Dani knew tonight was going to be chillier than it had been in weeks.

"We should move back inside," Dani said softly. Ava leaned into her.

"In a minute," Ava replied. Her voice was quiet, and it had Dani relaxing more as the sounds of the night started their evening concert.

Nights like these made it hard for Dani to imagine ever living anywhere else. She wasn't naive. She knew that eventually one of them would end up moving out of the house and starting their own life, independent from the family's home base. Dani's bet was on Ava mov-ing in with Grace in the next couple months. She didn't think Vini would leave completely, but Dani could see her globe-trotting with Jessica whenever she had a spare week where Aiden could hold down the fort. She was happy for her sisters, but that left Dani standing alone as the Williams Clan fractured and split.

She wasn't sure she was ready.

"Am I a good mom?" The question seemed to come out of nowhere, but Ava didn't miss a beat.

"One of the best I've ever known."

Dani looked over when one of Ava's hands slid over her own. Ava was looking at her, dark eyes warm and steadfast. There was no waver in her gaze. Dani smiled and turned her hand over. Their fingers slid together as they both held tight. Nothing else needed to be said, so they sat there in pleasant silence as the sky darkened, welcoming the night.

Dani should have known that the week wouldn't continue along so easily. Work today was the opposite of how it was yesterday. Clearly, she had jinxed herself by even thinking that the day had been quiet and easy. No, she needed to guard her thoughts against the universe, otherwise it would assume she needed a little more excitement in her life.

"Why is today so rough?" Natasha asked, her tone bordering on a whine as she collapsed into her chair. They had been going almost nonstop since clocking in, and she looked like a stiff wind might blow her over. Dani didn't feel much better herself. She'd barely had time to take a sip of water and pee before her pager went off and she was off down the hallway again.

"Cursed," she said as she leaned back in her chair. "We apparently pissed off the universe and now it's getting its revenge."

"Can it revenge softer? I can't feel my feet."

"You will tomorrow."

Natasha snorted softly but didn't deny Dani's words. It wasn't a threat. It was damn near a promise. Even with the best shoes, after a day like today, you were guaranteed to be sore and exhausted.

"So, hey," Natasha said, getting Dani's attention. "How are things with Zoey?"

When Dani gave her a sharp glance, Natasha laughed.

"I know you didn't think you two were being subtle." When Dani remained quiet, Natasha shook her head. "Mrs. P saw y'all holding hands outside the ice-cream parlor like a week ago, and Mrs. Susan was telling her how you two make swoony eyes at one another over your book club books."

"We don't make swoony eyes," Dani countered. "I'm too old to make swoony eyes at anyone."

"Girl, please. You're not even thirty yet and even if you were fifty, swoony eyes has no age limit." She looked Dani up and down. "You could have just told me you liked women too. I could have branched out and found someone else for you to go out with instead of Vernon. He says hi, by the way."

Dani snorted this time in amusement. "You can tell

him I said hi. Actually, it was on the date with him that I finally kind of realized what was up."

"So I heard. Flirting with someone else in front of your date is a bold strategy, but it seemed to work out for you, so congrats."

"I didn't flirt in front of him," Dani argued. When Natasha raised an eyebrow, she thought about it. "Okay, I didn't flirt in front of him on purpose. I didn't realize I *was* flirting until after the fact."

Natasha raised her arms over her head in a stretch. Dani winced when she heard something pop, but Natasha groaned in relief. "I needed that one." She grinned and wagged a finger at Dani. "It's all good, friend. Vernon still speaks highly of you, and I know you wouldn't do that on purpose. Nothing wrong with taking some time to figure things out. How did Jordan take the news that you're dating a woman now?"

Dani scratched the side of her cheek as she smiled awkwardly. "Well, there's the thing. I haven't told him yet. Not explicitly anyway." Jordan was a smart kid, so she didn't doubt he knew she was hanging out with Zoey more often. Dani had let the whole house know about book club. "I just haven't figured out the right time to say something."

"Girl, if you don't, just tell him. I'm sure he'll be happy for you."

Dani nodded. "Yeah, I guess."

"Unless you plan to date around," Natasha continued. "In that case, don't say anything. You don't want him getting attached and then you decide to date someone else or something. There's nothing worse than a parent that bounces around between partners."

Dani swallowed hard. That was almost word-for-word what Jacob had said. "Right. Wouldn't want to do that."

"Exactly," Natasha agreed, not realizing that Dani's thoughts had started to spiral. "It's a good thing Jacob settled down instead of being out with a different woman every night like a lot of these men."

The desk phone rang before Dani could say anything else. She watched Natasha pick it up and start talking, but her mind was too full to hear any words. The rest of her shift seemed to move slowly, like she was wading through invisible molasses. It wasn't until she was in her driveway that she realized she was supposed to have dinner at Zoey's place that night. With a sigh, she got out and headed into the house. She might as well change clothes since she was there. Right when she opened the door, Ava and Jordan skidded into view.

"What are you doing here?" Ava asked as she slid on her shoes. "I thought you were headed to Zoey's tonight."

"I am," Dani confirmed. "I was just going to grab a shower. Where are you guys headed?"

"Auntie Ava is taking me to meet Sam for laser tag."

Dani raised her eyebrows and looked over at Ava. "Isn't the closest one almost an hour away?"

Ava shrugged. "Sure, but I don't mind. Go grab a couple bottles of water from the kitchen, Jay." Ava watched him go before turning to Dani. "Sam's parents are going through a separation, so his mom asked if we would join them. Just to help get their minds off things."

Dani nodded. She had heard whispers in town about it, but had tried to stay out of the gossip. "If you're busy, I can cancel."

Ava waved her off. "Absolutely not. I got this. Go have fun with Zoey."

"Are you sure? I'm sure Zoey—"

"No," Ava said firmly. "You've canceled too many dates on people. Don't mess this up."

Jordan walked back into the room holding two bottles and once he had his shoes on, they quickly left, leaving Dani alone with the mess that was her own thoughts. By the time she was showered and walking up to Zoey's door, she could feel a headache coming on. The smile on Zoey's face when she opened the door fell when she saw Dani rubbing at her temples.

"Are you okay?" She stepped back and let Dani inside.

Dani smiled. "I'm okay. Just a little headache, thanks to a really busy day."

"Here, let me get you some pain medicine. Go ahead and sit on the couch. I ordered pizza, if that's alright."

"That's perfect," Dani called out as she collapsed on the sofa. She leaned her head back with a sigh and tried to clear her mind. When she heard footsteps coming back into the room, she lifted her head and squinted in Zoey's direction.

"I only have the powdered stuff," Zoey said with a grimace. "Mason bought some when he was here, but he didn't get the pills like I was hoping."

Dani took the offered drink and pain medicine. "Medicine is medicine to me as long as it helps." She ripped open the packet and poured the powder onto her tongue. The taste was hardly pleasant, but at least it should hit a little faster. She gulped down the water gratefully before feeling the couch dip down.

Zoey handed her a plate before dropping a couple slices onto it. Food did wonders for Dani's mood, but she couldn't completely shake the feelings that had settled over her. She knew Zoey was occasionally sneaking glances at her and she wanted to smile and say everything was fine, but she couldn't. She was floundering in the face of so many opinions and still smarting from her argument with Jacob. If not for Natasha's comments, she might have been able to overlook them, but what did it mean that they both practically said the same thing? Was Dani moving about all this the wrong way?

"I know you said you're okay," Zoey said, breaking their silence. "But are you sure? I'm a great listener if you need someone to talk to."

Dani wanted to, but she couldn't shake the feeling that this was too much too soon. She and Zoey were already entangled faster than she had ever planned. She had always told herself that it would be minimum six months of serious dating before Jordan ever got involved, and yet he was already entwined. Dani couldn't shake the feeling of what if this all went wrong?

What if it went right?

"No. I mean, yeah, I'm okay," Dani said finally as she looked up from her now-empty plate. The pizza had tasted good, but now that it was swallowed it sat heavy in her stomach. "I just have a lot on my mind."

Zoey nodded. "I can imagine." She picked up their empty plates and took them into the kitchen. Not wanting her to clean up alone, Dani picked up the pizza boxes and followed. They worked together in near silence, the only sounds coming from them walking around each other and putting things away. Dani was starting to learn Zoey's kitchen, and for some reason, that fact scared her. Getting too familiar was dangerous, especially because it meant that comfort could be ripped away.

When hands curled around her waist, Dani jumped slightly, tensing before she relaxed back into Zoey's familiar embrace.

"You know you can talk to me," she whispered in Dani's ear. Warmth brushed over her shoulder, making Dani shiver. It was a familiar feeling, though it didn't warm her as it usually did. She felt trapped, her thoughts centering on the what-ifs that had steadily grown louder. *What if this is all just temporary?*

"Dani, what if we—"

"I don't know if I am ready for a relationship." Dani hadn't meant to blurt out her words, but she had panicked not knowing how to give voice to her insecurities. The arms didn't withdraw, but Dani felt Zoey tense against her. She hated that she was having to bring all this up, but she would hate even more having to lie to Zoey and pretend to be okay. She had thought she was ready, but how could she bring someone else into the changing seasons that were her life?

"Is it..." Zoey trailed off as she pulled away. "Did I do something?"

Dani turned and shook her head. "No. You have been absolutely perfect."

"Then what's going on?" She asked, hurt and confusion clear on her face. They hadn't even talked about what this was between them and already Dani was causing her pain. *Maybe this all just needs to end now.*

"I don't know how to handle dating and raising a child." When Zoey looked at her in confusion, Dani felt something in her snap. "When Jordan was born, I was so afraid of getting things wrong. I second-guessed myself into barely leaving the house. All I could think about was what would happen if I did something wrong and he got hurt. Now, he's older, but I still have those same thoughts."

Zoey nodded along as she spoke, and Dani felt seen. "I mean, I get it as much as I can, given that I don't have kids. But, Dani, you are a damn good mom."

"Thank you," Dani said. "I do appreciate it, even if I don't believe it right now. I feel like everything has changed and is continuing to change so rapidly. I am failing epically to help ready him for the real world. He locked himself in his room for an entire day this past weekend and barely spoke to me."

"You know, when he came to me and talked about

his dad getting married and the baby being on the way, not once did he ever say that he thought you were failing him," Zoey said. She reached out and cupped Dani's cheek, her touch so soft, like Dani was something fragile. "Change is inevitable. But I think you are doing pretty good at riding it out."

"I'm afraid," Dani whispered finally. Zoey went quiet as she waited for Dani to say more. "Jordan feels like his dad is replacing him with a new wife and child, and I'm afraid that he will think I'm trying to replace him as well."

Zoey frowned. "He knows you wouldn't do that."

Dani sighed and shook her head. "I'm sure he knew his dad wouldn't either, until he did. Yet, here we are."

Zoey was silent for a moment, her thumb brushing softly over Dani's cheek. "So, what does this mean for you? For us?"

Dani knew what she wanted, but she just wasn't sure if now was the perfect time for her to be selfish. "I think maybe we should just remain friends."

She hated those words even as she let them fly. The greedy part of her wanted to grab them and stuff them down deep where no one would find them. Being "just friends" was a consolation prize that Dani didn't truly want. She wanted nights with Zoey in her bed and she wanted to wake up next to her the morning after. Being just friends would never be enough for Dani, and yet somehow, Dani was left with just that.

And the worst part, it was her who'd forced them into it.

Twenty-Two

"It's here!" Tiffany exclaimed, rushing up to the circulation desk and slamming her laptop on the counter. Zoey looked up briefly before looking at Tiffany.

"I have no idea what I'm looking at. Care to elaborate?"

Tiffany huffed but turned the computer around so she could read it. "It's the results from the board. I'm looking at my newest permanent coworker." Tiffany's grin was wide, but Zoey could hardly crack a smile. Not after being effectively dumped a couple days ago. Zoey hadn't realized you could be broken up with before you even officially started dating.

"It's the board item that we needed to get approval on in order to hire you full-time on a permanent basis. It finally came through and we are good to go."

That was fantastic news. Then again, did Zoey even want to stay in Peach Blossom? She had been so sure before, but that was when she thought she would have someone to share it with. Now, she was all alone—minus her few friends and book club. Getting back out on the road seemed daunting, but maybe it was the best course of action. She hadn't yet talked to Mason about the way things had gone because she didn't want to worry him, not after the conversation that they'd had last week.

Even though Dani had essentially pumped the brakes on their brewing relationship, she had still provided her with books that she thought would be helpful when dealing with the recent changes in Jordan's life. She had dropped them off at the Williams house the day after their failed date night. Dani had been there and although she was as beautiful as ever, she did look a little worse for wear. For a moment Zoey wondered if she was feeling the same way about the pause in their relationship. Did Dani regret it?

"I don't know," Zoey said slowly and gently, broaching the subject. "I've been talking to my brother and considering making a move to spend some time out where he is."

"What?" Tiffany's smile started to fall as she digested Zoey's words. "Why? I thought you were ready to settle down here."

"I was," Zoey assured her. "I suppose I still am, but I would need some time to myself to let my feelings for Dani fade away."

Tiffany crossed her arms. "But you can do that here. You don't need to leave town just because Dani was here first." Tiffany waved her hand at the computer screen.

"We secured funding specifically for you. You can't leave me so soon after that."

"Maybe they'll use the budget to hire someone who doesn't have a connection to the town, even if it was just in the form of another person," Zoey said. She hadn't thought seriously about where she might go if she didn't stay in Peach Blossom. There were plenty of small towns in Georgia that could be quaint places of peace. Maybe Zoey should try some of those before she made a decision.

"Wait, you're leaving?"

Zoey turned to look behind Tiffany and saw Jordan standing there with books in his hands. She hadn't expected to see him and couldn't help but look around to see if Dani was the one who brought him. She and Dani hadn't really talked or texted since book club. Zoey had wanted to reach out multiple times, but she had restrained herself.

"Hi, Jordan," Zoey said beckoning him to the counter. He walked up before placing the books on the counter. "Returning all of these already?"

He nodded. "Yeah. Thank you for helping me find them and letting me borrow them."

"You're totally welcome," Zoey said mustering up a small smile as she pulled the books closer to her.

"Are you leaving because of my mom?" His question nearly sent her reeling and Zoey had to fight hard not to let her surprise show on her face. Jordan was a very observant kid, and she knew she would need to play this very carefully.

"No. Your mom is a great person. She's been a really good friend to me," Zoey answered diplomatically. "Sometimes, things just don't work out the way we hope. That's all."

Jordan nodded slowly but he seemed to be thinking about something. Zoey and Tiffany exchanged looks before Tiffany excused herself and headed toward the office. "Do you like my mom?"

"Of course I do. She's a very nice person."

Jordan shook his head before moving closer to the counter. "No, I mean do you *like her* like her? Like, as a girlfriend?"

Zoey sucked in a sharp breath. She didn't know how to answer this. She didn't want to lie to him, but she also wasn't sure what Dani had really told him about them. She didn't want to overstep and cause trouble for Dani down the road.

"Yes," she finally answered, simply and honestly. "I like your mom a lot."

Jordan nodded as if he'd expected it, and maybe he had. Kids were very observant when they wanted to be. "I thought you did."

"Are you okay with that?" Zoey asked. She was genuinely curious to hear his thoughts. "I don't want you to feel like I'm trying to replace your dad, or that you aren't the center of your mom's world."

"I know, and I'm okay with it." Jordan smiled and Zoey felt almost effervescent. She hadn't expected to get Jordan's blessing to date his mom, but she could admit that the whole thing had impeccable timing. "It's actually a good thing, I think. She needs new friends but if you leave, we can't go with you."

"Jordan—"

"No, seriously," he said, cutting off her words. "For a while, my mom was just kind of existing. She was always fun and took me places, but other than that, she always just seemed sad. It wasn't until she started hanging out with you that she really started smiling. I want her to always be happy, and she's happy with you."

Zoey didn't know what to think about the declaration. On one hand, she wanted to simply fade into the background of Peach Blossom's populace. On the other, she wanted to be front and center—and hand in hand—with Jordan and Dani. That was the hardest part about trying to be self-aware. She knew she had an almost pathological need to be in a stable familial structure. Zoey wanted the family dream so much it almost made her teeth hurt. She wanted to get married, have kids, and maybe a pet or two. Sometimes, that was hard to find, even more so when you lived in a small town, or wanted to. But here, Zoey seemed to have found something that she couldn't help but want to cling to.

She didn't want to let Dani go.

"Jordan. Are you ready to go?"

Zoey looked up in time to see Dani walk around the corner. When their gazes meet, Dani came to a stop in the middle of the hallway. Time seemed to stand still as they stared at one another, and the sounds of the library faded away, leaving only one thought: Zoey wanted Dani and she would fight like hell to make this work.

"Not yet," Jordan said, his voice breaking through the fog Zoey seemed to have fallen into. She blinked quickly and looked away. Tiffany was looking back and forth between Dani and Zoey with a knowing smile on her face. She looked like she was enjoying some prime entertainment and if not for the way her mind was buzzing, Zoey would have told her to stop it.

"Zoey...hi." Dani spoke first, breaking the spell that had charmed Zoey into saying nothing at all. "I've been meaning to call you."

"Really?" Zoey couldn't help but ask. She hadn't meant to sound so hopeful, but days of no Dani in her life had left her feeling ravenous for even the smallest glimpse of her face. Having her whole and real in front of her was like a fever dream, and one that Zoey didn't quite want to wake up from. "What did you want to talk about?"

Dani glanced at Jordan before giving her a small smile. "Just some things. Maybe we could have dinner? If you want to."

"I do." Tiffany's snicker made Zoey want to elbow her, but she resisted. "You could come by mine if you want."

"That would be great," Dani said, her voice sounding achingly sincere. Her smile was little more than a slight twist of her lips, and yet it gave Zoey the type of hope that should be illegal. She had to curb her excitement. A simple dinner should not have her already planning out what to cook. "Are you free tonight? I know it's sort of short notice. Tomorrow works too."

Zoey jumped at the chance to talk so soon. It was better for her to get the talk out of the way as soon as possible, given how she tended to spiral when she was left to her own devices for too long. "Tonight works. I'm actually getting off in about thirty minutes, so we could do around eight if that works for you? I know it's sort of a late dinner."

Dani nodded. "Eight is perfect. I'll see you then."

"Right. See you…" Zoey trailed off as Dani and Jordan walked away from the desk. Zoey couldn't help the way her eyes traced Dani's frame, greedy for every little bit of her. When Dani turned back with a smile, Zoey couldn't help the twist of her lips as she gave a little wave. If not for Tiffany jostling her shoulder, she might have stood there staring at the door until her shift ended.

"So, what was that about you potentially leaving Peach Blossom?" Tiffany asked, her voice taking on a knowing tone. Zoey couldn't even deny it. She was foolishly letting her future location ride on whether or not this thing with Dani was salvageable. It should have left her unnerved that she cared this much and was willing to change things up just for a person who she'd only really ever kissed a couple times, and yet it just felt right. Mason would no doubt have had some choice words for her, but damn it, Zoey was a grown-ass woman. If she wanted to follow her heart and see where it led, she would. That was her decision and one she knew she would regret if she didn't take.

"I still might leave," Zoey said finally, not wanting to give Tiffany false hope even as her own took flight. "I can't make any promises."

Tiffany snorted softly. "Sure, friend. I'll go ahead and put in for new equipment for you. At least training you will be a breeze."

Twenty-Three

Dani was trying to keep it together as she drove back to the house. She hadn't gone into the library intending to walk out with a date for dinner at Zoey's, especially not after their last conversation. It hadn't even taken her a day to regret her words. She had barely gotten two steps from Zoey's front door before wanting to turn back around and tell Zoey she was just kidding. When Zoey had still shown up with books, ready to help out, Dani had given her a watery smile before spending the next couple hours talking to herself while immersed in a tub of water. If not for Ava banging on the door and needing to get in and ready for a dinner date with Grace, Dani might have stayed in there all night. She might have walked out looking like a prune with her shriveled-up fingers, but she had come away with the realization that she didn't want to let Zoey go so easily.

Bringing Jordan to the library to return the books had

been an easy excuse to come in and apologize. That was all she had intended to do. But when Dani was face-to-face with Zoey again, her mouth had run away with her and the next thing she knew, she had a couple hours to prepare to have one of the hardest conversations she'd had in a long while, certainly since she had to explain the birds and the bees to Jordan without sending them both running for the hills.

"Are you and Ms. Zoey going to hang out again?"

Jordan's question caught Dani off guard, and she glanced over at where he sat in the passenger seat of the car. His voice didn't give her any clue how he felt about it, so Dani decided to play it safe.

"Yeah. I'm going to have dinner with her tonight if that's okay with you." He shrugged but picked at his shorts, which was a telltale sign he had more to say. "Are you okay with that?"

Jordan shrugged again but spoke up this time. "That's fine. I like her."

"I know. We talked about—"

"Not like that," he said, quickly cutting her off. "And it's not that I *like her* like her anymore. I just think it's cool that she knows about gaming and stuff."

Dani didn't press the issue. "So, you're alright with me hanging out with her tonight and later on?"

"Yeah. You smile a lot more after book club, and her brother is pretty cool. He added me on my game, and we obliterated the other team when we did team battles.

If you and her stop being friends, he might stop playing and that would ruin my streak."

"Nice to know where your priorities are, kid," Dani said with a soft snort of amusement. As much as she sounded nonchalant, she was very much not on the inside. She could kick herself for thinking about making a sweeping decision before she even talked to Jordan. Isn't that what his dad had done? As much as she had wanted to do differently, at the end of the day she had almost botched this chance at communicating with Jordan to hear his thoughts. "But what if...what if I wanted to date Ms. Zoey? Like how Ava and Grace date."

Dani had racked her brain for weeks trying to figure out how to approach this subject, but at the end of the day, all she had come up with was to just do it. Rip the Band-Aid off and ride the wave of pain as it came.

"Okay."

The answer was simple to the point of causing Dani some confusion. *Okay? Just like that?* Was that really all Jordan had to say? It seemed so anticlimactic and yet, he was just sitting in his seat, totally unbothered by this huge revelation. How was it that Dani felt this major shift and yet for him it was just another Tuesday night?

"Well...okay then," Dani said, nodding. She looked back at the road as she turned onto their street. "Good talk." Beside her, Jordan snickered but she didn't bother calling him on it.

When they got to the house, Dani was relieved to see

Ava's car in the driveway. As soon as they got inside the house, she was at her sister's bedroom door.

"Ava? You in there?"

"Yeah." Ava's voice was muffled, and Dani opened the door slowly, only peeking in at first to make sure Grace wasn't in there too. When she saw Ava sitting at her desk, she sighed in relief and walked in before shutting the door behind her and locking it for good measure. Ava raised an eyebrow. "Are you about to murder me or something? I promise I didn't take your purse."

"I know you took it, don't even try that," Dani shot back as she walked over to the bed and dropped down onto it. "But this isn't about your sticky fingers. As long as you return it in the condition you pilfered it in, you'll live. I wanted to talk to you about something."

Ava's expression didn't change but she waved for Dani to go ahead. Dani took a deep breath in before speaking. She had to be prepared for tonight's dinner and when in doubt, she fell back on the familiar act of research until she felt she had a better handle on the situation and was equipped to deal with whichever direction things went in.

"I want to have sex with Zoey."

Silence met her words and Dani sat up with a jerk when she realized she had just come out with it. That wasn't what she had intended to say. It wasn't a lie. She did want to have sex with Zoey, but she had planned on easing into that by asking other questions first.

"Wow. Tell me how you really feel," Ava quipped, making Dani scowl. Ava held up her hands in surrender before a smile split her face. "So, you finally decided to come over to the cool side of the Kinsey scale. Welcome. We have flags and the best agenda ever."

Dani couldn't help but chuckle, and shook her head. "Thanks, sis. But I do actually need advice." She sighed and looked away, feeling strangely young somehow. "Other than myself, I've never been with another woman so I'm kind of at a loss about how to approach things."

"Well, first things first, are you guys just messing around or is there something more there?"

It was a valid question. "We're having dinner tonight. I know Zoey had wanted to date before I put the brakes on things, but now I don't know if she's still going to want that or if I've royally fucked myself there."

Ava sat back in her chair. "I don't know about that. She seemed pretty into you and that doesn't just go away like that. I think if you sincerely apologize and just explain that you were suffering from a bad case of 'doing what you thought you should instead of what you wanted to' she'll probably forgive you."

Dani had planned on apologizing as it was and giving a full explanation of where her head was at. She just hoped it was enough. "Okay. I'll do that. But what if things do go well? How do I like..." Dani trailed off. She raised her eyebrows, trying to get Ava to get the hint.

Ava snorted and shook her head. "Approaching a woman really isn't much more different than a guy, especially given you both want each other. I'm assuming you two have already kissed." When Dani nodded, she continued, "Well, how did that go?"

Dani couldn't help but smile when she thought about the last kiss she and Zoey had shared. "It was good."

"Clearly, based on that reaction," Ava said, rolling her eyes.

"Right, but what if I do it wrong and she thinks it's not worth it? I've only ever had sex with men. What if I suck at women-on-women sex? Looking at lesbian porn just left me with a complex about shaving or not."

Ava rubbed her forehead. "You've said the word *sex* one too many times for me to deal with this alone, and I never wanted to know about any of your nighttime viewing activities. I'm calling in a reinforcement."

Dani tried to focus on figuring out who Ava was calling and ignore the downward spiral of her thoughts. When the phone connected and she heard Vini's voice, Dani wasn't sure whether to feel horrified or relieved.

"Ava, we talked about this. Time zones."

"Dani wants to have sex with Zoey. Tonight."

There was a beat of silence before Vini spoke again, her voice sounding far more awake than before. "Well, hell. Lead with that next time." There was the sound of shuffling and then the closing of a door before Vini spoke again. "Okay. So, this is serious then? You finally jumped ship?"

Dani chuckled. "I don't know about all that, but I like Zoey, and I think there's something there that I want to lean into."

"And you think about being with her physically?" When Ava asked, Dani gave her an incredulous look. "Hey, just making sure that you aren't confusing friendship for attraction, and what you want to lean into is her pus—"

"She's got a point." Vini spoke up, cutting off Ava's words. "Are you sure you aren't just lonely?"

Dani wanted to protest, but the questions were valid, and she knew that. She needed to think carefully about things to keep from hurting not only Zoey but the people they shared. If things didn't work out between them, it could make things awkward. Still, when she thought about kissing Zoey and going even further than that, her body filled with heat. The reaction confirmed what she had felt. And even beyond, she thought about just relaxing with Zoey on the couch with a book and nothing but time. That was almost as attractive as the sex. That type of contentment had her sighing wistfully.

"Yeah, Vin, she's got it bad," Ava said, breaking Dani from her fantasies. When she looked up, Ava had a smile on her face that looked equal parts fond and disgusted. "You should have seen her face when she thought about Zoey. I've never seen so many emotions at one time. It was wonderfully disgusting and I'm happy for you."

Dani rolled her eyes but didn't deny it. She didn't know what her face had done, but if it moved along the conversation, all the better. "Thanks, I guess. So now will you two help me figure out how to do this?"

Ava rolled her chair closer. "Of course. But first you have to promise to not tell us anything."

"Agreed," Vini chimed in. "No details. As long as you're happy, we're happy for you."

Dani snorted. It was hilarious that they were the ones saying that stipulation, but she nodded in agreement. "Fine. Just help a girl out and then I'll keep my bliss quiet."

Ava laughed not unkindly. Dani wasn't sure if she was making a bigger deal of things, but she knew she wanted to get things right this time.

Twenty-Four

Zoey had been in motion the moment she stepped foot inside the house. She had never cleaned so fast in her life and now that the house looked as good as it could by her hand, she was trying to focus on doing the same for herself. She knew she only had so much time to prepare what with dinner baking in the stove. She had sent a text to Dani with a time and then promptly tried not to freak the fuck out. *I am an adult. Having someone come over shouldn't have me this out of sorts.* With a sigh, she finished dragging the net against her skin, enjoying the soft scratches as she imagined a familiar hand gliding over that exfoliated bit of skin in appreciation.

Getting dressed presented another dilemma because what the fuck was she supposed to wear for dinner in her own house? Usually, if she were alone, she would toss on some pajamas and call it a day. If Tiffany was over, she'd either do the same or a pair of sweats and a T-shirt. But this was a date, *the* date if she was being real. Tonight would either make or break a potential relationship with Dani because as much as Zoey wanted this, she knew that she couldn't be the only one trying. She had learned her lesson once about being the sole person trying to make things work and it had done nothing but left her single and needing months of therapy.

It had been an unfortunate situation, but she had learned, and she knew better now how to identify those people-pleasing parts of her that would act against her best interests if she let them. She knew she and Dani needed to have actual conversations and not leave things to chance and hope they lucked into something healthy enough to be long-term, especially with a child involved. Still, even with the internal pep talk, Zoey still wasn't sure she was ready, especially not when there was a knock on the door and opening it led to coming face-to-face with Dani. Zoey couldn't help the way her eyes raked over Dani's slender frame, taking in the tight long-sleeve shirt that dipped at a waist that made Zoey want to reach out and grab, and the loose slacks that seemed to go on for miles, showcasing long legs.

"Hey." Dani's voice was unusually subdued, and Zoey had to grip the doorknob to keep from backing up. Her pulse was beating double time but Zoey forced herself to smile and gestured for Dani to come in.

"Hey. Perfect timing. The food is ready to come out of the oven." Zoey pushed some false cheer into her voice to cover up for how reedy it was. After Dani walked in,

Zoey took a moment to breathe deep before she turned around. She almost needed a few more breaths because damn it if Dani didn't make her want, just by standing in the middle of her living room. "You can take a seat at the table. It's set up and I'll bring the food over."

Dani nodded before pausing. "Is there anything I can help with?" She reached into her purse. "I brought a bottle of wine, but didn't want to make you think I was trying to get us drunk before talking or anything."

Zoey's smile felt more genuine when she reached for the bottle. Maybe it was rude, but she was happy to see that Dani was perhaps just as nervous as her. It made Zoey feel less alone in just how fervently she wanted this to work. When their fingers brushed, she looked up, locking eyes with Dani. That feeling—the flush of attraction and the slight zap of electricity in their touch—wasn't something that could be explained away. It needed to be confronted and either denied or confirmed.

"If you want to grab a couple wineglasses from the cabinet over there, that would be great." *And it will give me time to get myself together.* Zoey was momentarily granted a reprieve when Dani moved in the direction she was pointing. She escaped back into the kitchen to take a couple of calming breaths before grabbing the food and bringing it to the table. Dani was standing by the table, smiling softly down at the glasses and Zoey almost stubbed her toe on the wall. Her stumbling must have alerted Dani to her presence because she looked up at her, soft smile still on her face.

"Smells delicious," Dani said when Zoey placed the casserole dish on the table.

"I hope you're hungry." When Dani looked back up at her, Zoey swallowed hard. "It's nothing special but—"

"It's special because you made it," Dani cut in. She moved to sit, not realizing she was single-handedly destroying Zoey's plans of not falling any harder for her. Zoey quickly followed, sitting across from her before realizing she might have made a calculated mistake. How the hell was she supposed to focus on food with Dani sitting there across from her looking like a five-course meal? Thinking quickly, she uncorked the wine and held out the bottle.

"Wine?"

Zoey busied herself with filling their glasses as Dani scooped out a helping of lasagna for both of them and then the salad. They began eating, neither saying anything. Zoey wasn't sure how to bring up the conversation she knew they needed to have. Should she just lead with how much she liked Dani and see how she felt? Should she talk about why she was wary about things? How did you talk about a past relationship where you were taken advantage of without trying to seem like a victim or like you weren't over it? She was over it, even if it still had rippling effects.

"So, I want to apologize." Zoey looked up at Dani's words. Of all the openings, that wasn't even close to what she was expecting. Dani was holding her wineglass, though it still looked as full as it had been when Zoey first poured them. She was looking down at the ruby-red liquid as it swirled slightly in her cup. As if sensing Zoey's eyes on her, she paused and looked up. "Why do you look so stunned?"

Zoey shook herself before replying. She hadn't been aware that her surprise was written all over her face. "I just wasn't expecting you to do that."

Dani cocked her head to the side. "What? Apologize?" When Zoey nodded, she furrowed her brow. "Why not? I was the one who put the brakes on things, and pretty abruptly at that. I should have talked to you instead of just spouting off at the mouth and leaving. I get onto Ava about doing that, but now I realize who she probably got it from."

Zoey chuckled when Dani's lips turned up in a wry smile. She did appreciate the apology, even if she didn't think it was necessary. "You didn't have to, but thank you. I have to ask though. Is your hesitance really just because of Jordan or is it also because I'm a woman?"

Dani froze for a moment before she leaned back in her chair. Her gaze dropped to the table and Zoey gave her a moment to answer instead taking another few bites of her own food as she waited.

"Truthfully, it's both," Dani said finally. She looked back up at Zoey. "But I'm more worried that I'll…" She trailed off, looking away again and this time when Zoey looked closer, it was almost like Dani was embarrassed.

"You'll what?" she said, prompting Dani to finish the sentence she had started.

Dani sighed and set her glass down. "Worried that I'll do something wrong. I'll ask the wrong question or make some assumption that shows how completely out of my depth I am when it comes to dating women—to dating you." Maybe the confession should have given Zoey pause, but instead it made her feel lighter. She couldn't help the smile that spread on her lips. When Dani saw her, she rolled her eyes. "You are looking way too smug."

"Not smug," Zoey said. "Just realizing that you really like me."

"Of course I do. Why would you be bothering with me if I didn't?"

The question hit a bit too close to home, but it was probably better to get it all out there. "Because I did before. Not with you, but with another woman I liked." Dani's confusion was clear on her face, so Zoey continued explaining. "I, well, not dated, but was around a woman before who I liked even though she never explicitly said she liked me. I had hoped that...well, she wasn't interested in me like that. Not really."

"She used you." Hearing Dani say it so bluntly had Zoey biting back excuses. It was hard admitting she was used, even after coming to terms with it. "Yeah. I wanted to be a good friend and thought that we were on the same page about the direction of our relationship, but we weren't. Mason says it's because I seek out the stability we didn't really have."

Dani looked at her for a moment. "Is that why you like me? Because I'm stable?"

Zoey frowned. "No. I mean, yes, but not like that. I'm not trying to use you to fulfill some hole in myself. I like you because you're funny, and smart, and have really great taste in books." When Dani snorted out a laugh, Zoey gave her a tentative smile. "I won't lie, I do want the picket fence—type family, but I wouldn't just go after anyone to have it. I like you because you're you."

It was a couple minutes before Dani finally answered her, lips pulling apart in a hesitant smile. "I like you because you're you too. I'm not using you as some sort of experiment or a way to get more excitement in my life. I don't want to lie to you. I'm still figuring out if I'm bisexual or lesbian. Both? Neither?"

Zoey chuckled, understanding how confusing it can be to figure things out. "I get it."

"Good. Great," Dani said with a sigh. Zoey saw her shoulders drop and realized just how tense Dani had been. "I never really dated much. I never felt the need or saw the appeal of trying to get to know someone, but with you, I want to know everything."

"I'll tell you everything," Zoey said without thinking. Blinking quickly, she realized she had been leaning forward, almost dipping the sleeve of her blouse into her plate. "You can ask me whatever you want."

Dani nodded slowly, her smile widening. "You can do the same with me. I won't promise to have all the answers yet, but I can promise that I like you. This isn't some passing phase for me." Her gaze shifted heat in them, seeming to ignite. "And when I say I like you, I mean in every way. My feelings are in no way platonic when I think about you."

Zoey reached for her wine and took a large sip that did nothing to wet her suddenly dry mouth. She had hoped Dani liked her like that, but to hear it so bluntly was doing things for her that should have been illegal. The confirmation that they were on the same page with their feelings lifted a weight off her shoulders.

"That's great. Me too. When I think about you, I mean," she said, stumbling over her words. Dani's smile shifted into something lighter, and Zoey nearly jumped out of her chair to run around the block in triumph. "So...you and me?"

Dani leaned forward and put her hand palm up on the table between the two of them. Zoey looked at it before reaching out to place her hand in Dani's. Her touch was soft and the warmth of it bled into Zoey's skin. Brown met brown and Zoey felt her breath hitch.

"You and me."

Twenty-Five

Dinner had been a resounding success, at least in Dani's opinion. She had gotten out everything she had been feeling and had even learned more about where Zoey was coming from. She had hoped to, but she didn't want to seem like she was prying into Zoey's past or mining for information without offering any of her own. She hoped she had explained where she was coming from enough to give some assurance that she was in this for real.

"Here's your coffee," Zoey said. Dani looked up in time to have a cup placed in front of her on the coffee table. She smiled gratefully when Zoey sat down beside her with her own cup. Dani picked it up, breathing in the nutty scent like it was a lifeline. She was a bit tired, but she desperately didn't want the night to be done yet. "So, how is Jordan with all of this? I know you mentioned before he was having trouble with his dad getting married."

Dani took a deep sip before answering. "With you and

me, he's fine—encouraging even. I think my dad lets him have extra gaming time when I'm not around so he's eager to push me out of the house as much as possible."

Zoey chuckled. "I can see that. Well, I'm glad that he's okay with this. I don't want to make things weird for him considering."

Warmth filled Dani's chest at Zoey's concern. It solidified her feelings about taking things further with Zoey and while she was sure no one would love Jordan quite like she did, Dani was happy that he and Zoey at least had an already-formed friendship outside of her.

"No weirdness at all," Dani confirmed before taking another sip of her coffee. She eyed Zoey over the rim of the mug, gaze drifting down to the open V-neck of her blouse. It was so novel to see Zoey outside of her usual T-shirt, jeans, and cardigan. As much as Dani loved that cardigan, she couldn't help but admire this new Zoey in her loose blouse that draped perfectly over umber skin. When she brought her gaze back up to meet Zoey's, Dani couldn't help but smile at being caught staring.

"What?" Zoey asked. "Why are you staring at me?"

Dani shrugged. "You're just gorgeous. That's all."

Zoey giggled before leaning over to put her mug on the table. "If you were anyone else, I'd think you were flirting with me."

"I am," Dani said simply, not bothering to mince words. "Is it working?"

Zoey sat back, her head cocking to the side as she peered at Dani from behind her glasses. "Yes."

Not one to miss an opportunity, Dani leaned forward to put her mug back on the table and followed through with the motion until she was close enough to feel Zoey's heat. She lifted her hand, trying to ignore the way it shook slightly. The first touch of Zoey's skin against the palm of her hand was enough to have her sure just how much she wanted this. Zoey's eyes were still open, twin pools of warm brown drawing her in like gravity. They only closed when their lips met, and Dani let her own eyes slip closed as she took in the feeling.

Zoey's lips were soft and a little chapped, but that only added to the realness. Dani had expected the kiss to feel different, and in a way it did. It felt so much *more* than what she had experienced, even when she was in the throes of passion with her previous lovers. Those touches had nothing on this, and she found herself pressing closer, trying to take in everything as if someone was going to come by and stop her. Maybe it was because she was so used to her sisters or Jordan barging in and interrupting her, but she kissed Zoey with a restless fervor, reaching up to cup both of Zoey's cheeks. It wasn't until she felt Zoey's body tip that Dani realized she had been nearly pressing her down onto the couch.

"Fuck, I'm so sorry," Dani said, easing up and helping Zoey to rise back into a seated position. She tried to ignore the heat of Zoey's hands on her waist. "I sort of lost myself there."

Zoey's glasses were slightly askew on her face and her lips were shiny with spit, but she didn't look the least bit upset. "Please don't apologize." Before Dani could say anything, Zoey pressed their lips together again, mirroring the hunger Dani felt inside and making her shiver. Her stomach swooped as she realized she wasn't the only one who might be desperate for more.

Apologies forgotten, Dani let herself go with the vibe, running her greedy fingers over the soft skin of Zoey's neck and smiling at her shudder. She pressed fingertips over velvet skin, stealing them under the fabric of Zoey's blouse.

"How far do you want this to go?" Zoey asked against her lips. Dani would be lying if she said she hadn't wanted this. Part of her was nervous, like she had been the first time she had lain with anyone, but another part of her was giddy with excitement. Her pulse beat against her skull in time with the wave of her arousal. They all seemed to be pushing for more. She wanted to taste the salt of Zoey's skin against her tongue and know just how she looked when she came. With a jolt, Dani realized she could have that now.

"Whatever you'll give me," Dani said in response, pressing chaste kisses to Zoey's lips and smiling when she chased her for more. Zoey's lips turned down in a disgruntled frown when Dani kept her lips away. "I want everything."

Zoey's gaze went molten behind her glasses and there was a split second when Dani thought she might have taken things too far. Abruptly, Zoey stood. Her hands came up to the buttons on her blouse as she turned away. She had only taken a few steps before she paused and looked at Dani over her shoulder.

"Well, are you coming or not?"

Dani blinked quickly before hopping up off the couch. "I wasn't sure if that was an invitation or not. I didn't want to assume."

Zoey smirked. "Feel free to assume all over me."

Dani followed her like a dancer following the most exquisite song. By the time she stepped into Zoey's bedroom, Zoey's blouse had fallen past her shoulders and when she turned to face Dani, she tossed it to the side. Dani didn't stop moving until she was again pressed against Zoey. At Zoey's prodding, she lifted her shirt up and over her head, letting it fall at their feet. Zoey's hands flitted over her skin leaving bursts of heated pleasure. When they kissed again, Dani shivered at how lush it all felt. It was rare she had a chance to be so unrushed and she reveled in it now.

Zoey's hands brushed against Dani's stomach before gripping the waistband of her pants. "Is this still okay?"

Dani nodded quickly before gripping Zoey's face again and pressing their lips tighter. Zoey's lips parted easily, letting Dani flit inside for a taste even as she groaned when those wicked fingers undid her jeans. The snap of the button seemed to throw things in overdrive and when Dani finally came up for air, they were both left in panties and bras, laid out on Zoey's bed. The air was cool against Dani's skin, but she barely felt it with Zoey covering her like the perfect weighted blanket, real and solid. Their legs tangled together and when Zoey shifted, Dani's breath caught in her throat at the thigh that pressed against her cunt, only fabric keeping them separated.

"Fuck, you're so hot," Dani panted out as she dug her fingers against Zoey's back. "How are you so hot?"

Zoey chuckled, her glasses long discarded, giving Dani an uninterrupted view of the heat in her gaze. "Lesbian."

Dani didn't know how else to respond other than to pull Zoey down in agreement. She fastened her lips to the skin of Zoey's neck, nipping there and enjoying the rumbled moan that followed her actions. She pressed her thumb under Zoey's jaw to angle her head up so she could get to more of that fragrant skin. The pulsing need between her thighs was growing stronger and Dani couldn't help but press her hips up to get more of that pressure. Zoey's chuckles should have been warning enough of what was coming, but when Dani felt fingers slip between her thighs and press against her covered cunt, she groaned against Zoey's neck.

"Is this alright?"

Dani nodded frantically, dropping her outside leg open and giving Zoey more space to work. She snaked a hand around Zoey's back to unclip her bra and felt triumphant when she managed to get it undone with little fuss. Her victory soon took a back seat to the feeling of questing fingers pushing the fabric of her panties aside before teasing up the lips of her. Dani muffled the sound of her moan against the swell of Zoey's breasts huffing out several breaths as those wicked fingers played her body like a well-loved instrument.

"There you go," Zoey whispered hotly against Dani's forehead. Her voice sounded so awed and appreciative that it hooked on something in Dani's chest making her breathe faster. When a finger slid inside of her with no hesitation, Dani sucked hard at the nipple in her mouth. The feelings emanating from between her thighs was enough to leave her gasping, but she didn't want to lie there and let Zoey do all the work. Or have all the fun. "Does that feel good?"

"Jesus," Dani panted releasing Zoey's nipple and looking up at her. "Are you always this vocal?"

Zoey tilted her head as she shifted to leaning on her free arm. "I have to stay quiet enough at my job, so I like being able to talk when I can. Do you not like it?" The small thread of insecurity was unacceptable to Dani, and she reached up to wrap an arm around Zoey's shoulders drawing her back down so they could kiss. She lost a little of her gentleness with each swipe of Zoey's tongue against her own and when they separated again, they were both out of breath.

"I fucking love it," Dani answered, not forgetting the question. "Talk to me some more."

Zoey chuckled, her eyes half-lidded as she peered down at Dani. Nothing gave her away until Dani felt another finger sliding between the lips of her pussy. The stretch was familiar and yet not. She had touched herself like this so many times, but it was different to have Zoey there, carving a space inside her as surely as she had carved a space in Dani's life. Feeling the need to make Zoey understand, Dani slid her own hand down until she could dip between Zoey's legs and feel the wet heat staining her panties. Perhaps she should have felt cautious about touching another woman for the first time like this, but all she could feel was a gluttonous need to see Zoey's face go slack in pleasure.

"You don't have—"

"Shut up and let me make you come," Dani said, interrupting Zoey's words. Before Zoey could reply, Dani gripped the back of her neck and brought their lips together again.

They moved together, fingers thrusting and matching the tempo of their tongues as they danced together from one mouth to another. Dani marveled at how lush Zoey felt inside, quickly pressing a second and third finger in when she loosened with pleasure. Moans and groans were swallowed by heated kisses and when Zoey groaned softly, Dani almost crowed. Zoey's fingers paused and her muscles went loose, pressing Dani down more. Dani chuckled and pressed kisses against Zoey's cheek until she lifted her head and gave Dani a glare.

"Don't look so smug."

Dani grinned wide. "How can you tell how I'm looking without your glasses?"

Zoey rolled her eyes before shifting up. "I'm not that blind. Besides, I can practically smell it on you." Dani opened her mouth to respond, but when fingers thrust back into her, all she could do was gasp. It was Zoey's turn to smirk. She moved then, pressing Dani's leg to the bed with her thigh and tucking her free hand around the top of Dani's head. "Shut up and come on my fingers."

Dani gasped out a laugh at her own words being

thrown back to her even as she gripped the covers in one hand and Zoey's waist with the other. The thrust of Zoey's fingers was firm and when her thumb circled Dani's clit, the added stimulation made her jerk into the motion.

"Oh, fuck," she groaned as she threw her head back, pushing against Zoey's hold. It was secure, the strength enough to push her that much higher. When Zoey leaned in to whisper heated dirty words against the sensitive shell of her ear, Dani knew she was a goner. When her orgasm hit, her body locked up and her breath slammed to a stop before rushing out of her in a tense cry. It felt like flying, her mind catching on the breeze of climax and taking flight before slamming her back into her body. When she could finally hear, she almost lost it again at Zoey's words.

"There you go, baby. You're so gorgeous when you come. I can't wait to taste you."

Dani sucked in a breath. "Are all librarians as good at sex talk as you?"

Zoey smiled, her eyes crinkling up in mirth. "I wouldn't know. We don't usually sit around trading words to say during sex." She leaned in to brush her lips over Dani's. "But I don't mind telling you more that I've come up with."

Dani smiled as she let go of the covers and cupped her hand around Zoey's cheek. "I want to hear everything."

Twenty-Six

Zoey had become accustomed to waking up alone, so when she woke up with a weight in her arms, her eyes slammed open before her brain fully came online. She looked around for a moment before turning her head and seeing a mass of hair. Memories flooded back into her mind and when she realized who it was lying on her arm, she couldn't stop herself from smiling. Somehow, she had managed to fall asleep with Dani in her arms and stay asleep through the night. She was notorious for not being able to fall asleep with someone in her bed and this seemed like the final thing to fall into place.

Last night had been…well, magical. Zoey wasn't some type of sex god charming maidens in her bed at every turn, but she had had her fair share of amorous moments. None of them had compared to last night. She hadn't ex-pected Dani to be so forward or so ready to jump into sex with another woman, given her recent revelations, but Zoey had never been so happy to be proven wrong. Dani had fallen against her with the type of hunger that nearly left Zoey speechless. When Zoey closed her eyes, the memory of Dani's face dipping between her thighs had her stomach clenching in renewed arousal.

A groan beside her had Zoey's heart lurching and she turned to watch Dani slowly wake up. Dani turned on her arm, head coming up as she looked around. When her sleep-addled brown eyes met Zoey's, she smiled softly, sending butterflies skittering in Zoey's stomach.

"Good morning." Dani's voice was scratchy and deeper than it was normally. It washed over Zoey pleasantly.

"Morning." Taking a chance, Zoey leaned in, pressing a chaste kiss against Dani's lips. When she pulled back, Dani's eyes were closed again but she had a little smile on her face that Zoey couldn't help but kiss again. "You are not allowed to look this cute when you wake up."

Dani snorted before resting her head back on the pillow and peering up at Zoey. "Look who's talking." She looked so comfortable lying there that Zoey just wanted to stay in bed with her all day. A glance at her clock let her know that she had a couple free hours before she needed to get ready for work. "Do you have to work today?"

"How did you know what I was thinking?" Zoey settled back down before throwing an arm over Dani's waist. "Are you secretly psychic?"

"If I was, it would make being a nurse so much easier," Dani said. She shifted, moving closer to Zoey. She looked so soft that Zoey had to reach out and touch. She brushed the back of her hand over Dani's cheek before leaning over and kissing her. "Morning breath."

"I don't give a fuck." Dani burst out in laughter and Zoey leaned back in confusion.

Dani shook her head. "It's just so fun hearing you curse when normally you're in your librarian mode." She kissed Zoey quickly before pushing up to sit. "But seriously, do you have to work today? I don't want to make you late."

Zoey groaned and pressed her face into her pillow before looking at Dani from the corner of her eye. "I do have work, but for the first time ever I want to play hooky and call in sick."

Dani chuckled before moving to stand beside the bed. Zoey turned to look at her more fully when she reached down to pull off the oversize T-shirt Zoey had let her borrow to sleep in. Seeing her standing there so unself-conscious in her nudity did things to Zoey and she shifted to move closer. Dani snorted and took a step away from the bed, staying just out of reach.

"Where are you going?" Zoey asked, trying to keep her gaze on Dani's face and not on her pert breasts and dark nipples that just called out to be touched and teased. "Do you need to leave?"

Dani smiled and put her hand on her hip, cocking it to the side. "Yes, eventually. But more, I need to get you up and out, so you aren't late to work. Can't have the town blaming me if their favorite librarian doesn't open the library up on time."

Zoey wanted to say that the town would forgive her

if they knew the siren she had standing in front of her, but she knew Dani was right. She needed to get up and get moving, otherwise she would spend all day buried in Dani's warmth. She groaned and moved to stand.

"Is you being right going to be a permanent thing?" Zoey asked, smiling to take the sting off her words. Dani cocked her head to the side before holding out a hand.

"Probably." Zoey took Dani's hand, pulling her against her. Their lips met again in a soft kiss before Dani pulled back to give her a sly smile. "But I think we should have some time to shower together. Right?"

Zoey didn't bother responding, instead cupping Dani's cheek and pulling her back into a kiss as she walked her back toward the bathroom door.

"Well, hello there stranger," Tiffany called out as she walked over to the circulation table. Zoey looked up, giving her a quizzical look.

"Stranger? I literally saw you yesterday."

"True, but it sounded fun to say." Tiffany walked by, heading to the office. When she got back, Zoey was reviewing the returned books as she geared up for sorting and moving them back onto their shelves. "How's the morning been?"

Zoey shrugged before answering. "Fine. It's been quieter than usual but I'm sure that'll change after lunch." She glanced at Tiffany. "How was yesterday? Sorry I left in kind of a hurry."

Zoey hadn't had to ask Tiffany twice about leaving a

little earlier than usual to prepare for dinner with Dani. It wasn't something Zoey planned to make a habit, though now she more than likely wouldn't need to since they'd sorted everything out. Zoey couldn't help but smile at the thought of how well they had sorted things out last night and then again in the shower that morning. She had never considered herself to be an uptight person, but she couldn't deny that the number of orgasms she'd had definitely contributed to how relaxed she now felt. She wasn't even stressed out about her looming deadline.

"What is this look on your face right now?"

Tiffany's question shook Zoey from her memories, and she quickly looked back at her laptop, avoiding Tiffany's stare. "I don't know what look you're talking about."

Zoey felt Tiffany move closer but forced her gaze to stay on the work in front of her. She actually did have tasks to finish before she left for the day. Plus, she wasn't sure if she was ready to divulge about last night. As much as she wanted to scream it from the top of the rafters, she and Dani hadn't discussed how they would handle people's comments. Zoey wasn't worried about anyone side-eyeing them. Peach Blossom was as progressive as a town could be, but even so, that didn't mean everyone wanted to be "out" with things. And with Dani just now figuring things out about herself, Zoey didn't want to force her from any proverbial closets before she was ready.

"So, have you thought about the position?"

Zoey snapped out of her own thoughts and glanced over at Tiffany. "The position?"

Tiffany put her hands on her hips and gave Zoey a hard look that Zoey was sure she didn't deserve. "The permanent position here. At the library? The one I put my blood, sweat and tears into pushing through the board?"

"Oh," Zoey replied, remembering the last conversation they'd had about it. With a sheepish look, Zoey ducked her head. "I hadn't thought about it actually. I kind of... forgot."

Tiffany's mouth flopped open as she gaped at Zoey in disbelief. "You forgot about it? Are you fucking kidding me? After all that work I put into it, you just up and forgot?" For a moment, Zoey wondered if she should move all of the books out of firing range. She wouldn't be surprised if Tiffany grabbed one and chucked it at her. Instead, Tiffany sighed. "I know you've been all up Dani's ass lately, but I need you to remove your head from her sphincter and remember that there are other things to think about."

Zoey winced. She hadn't realized she was that bad lately. "I'm sorry, Tiff."

Tiffany eyed her for a moment before shaking her head and smiling. "It's fine. I know you're working double time to show the sexy single mama that you are the perfect woman for her, so I can forgive you this time."

"Yeah, about that," Zoey said before trailing off.

Tiffany gave her an incredulous look. "Don't tell me you're giving up already? We can always come up with a new plan."

Zoey shook her head, halting Tiffany's words. "No,

not giving up. Dani and I had dinner last night, remember? We've already talk about everything."

Tiffany's eyes widened. "Okay...and?"

Zoey shrugged, though she felt anything but nonchalant. She couldn't stop the smile that spread across her face. "We decided to give it a try."

"'It'?"

"Being together," Zoey clarified. When Tiffany let out a loud squeal, Zoey shushed her quickly even while she felt her smile widen. Thankfully, there weren't that many patrons in the library, but still it would set a bad example if the librarians were the ones being disruptive. Still, Zoey couldn't help but warm at Tiffany's enthusiastic response to hearing about the change in her and Dani's relationship status. "You're more excited about this than I am."

Tiffany waved her words away. "I know that's a lie. I knew something was different about you when I came in. It's the happiness. It's written all over your face."

There was nothing to say to that. Zoey was happy and she didn't care who knew that, but she couldn't resist giving Tiffany a hard time. "You know what would make me really happy? If you would help me sort these returns."

Tiffany rolled her eyes. "Whatever. I know you're over the moon about things. Maybe next time your brother is in town, we can have a double date and you can officially introduce me to him."

Normally, Zoey would push back about that, but she was feeling entirely too good right now to care about the implosion that would be introducing her two favorite people. "Sure. Why the hell not." When Tiffany's eyes widened, Zoey couldn't help but chuckle.

"Damn. Dinner must have gone really well for you to be saying that. So, who did who?" Tiffany asked, waggling her eyebrows.

It was Zoey's turn to roll her eyes. "We're both women. We both did each other." She froze when she realized she had walked into that trap. Tiffany snickered.

"Well, food for you both. Nothing wrong with a little bump and grind to seal the deal."

Zoey shook her head though she didn't disagree. Her cellphone buzzing caught her eye, and when she realized it was Dani, Zoey smiled. She didn't hesitate to answer it. "Dani. Hey." When Tiffany made kissy faces in front of her, Zoey swatted at her before turning away so she could focus on the phone. "What's up? Is everything okay?"

"Everything is fine," Dani reassured. "I just made the mistake of coming home when the house was up and now they want you to come to dinner tonight. Be warned. It's most likely going to be an interrogation."

"Oh, should I be worried?"

"They're mostly harmless. But don't let Ava push you around, otherwise you'll never get the upper hand with her." Zoey giggled at Dani's warning. "Vini's still out of the country, so you won't have to deal with her yet. Easing in one sister at a time is probably the best strategy as is."

Zoey wasn't sure how to take that, but she figured if Dani could handle her brother, Mason, then Zoey could handle questions from Dani's family. Zoey also couldn't help her smile at the thought of sitting down to a meal at Dani's side. It meant a lot that she was already being invited over for meals instead of being hidden away like some dirty little secret.

"Do you want me to come for dinner?" Zoey asked. "I don't want you to feel pressured, like you have to announce us before you're ready."

"Of course, I want you to come for dinner," Dani said. There was muffled talking on the other line. "I don't feel pressured at all. I get to brag about bagging the hottest librarian. No offense to Tiffany."

Warmth infused Zoey and if not for having an audience, she would probably be giggling like a schoolgirl whose crush just looked her way. "Then sure. I would love to come to dinner tonight. Should I bring anything?"

"Just yourself." There was more commotion across the line before Dani spoke up again. "I have to go. See you tonight. Seven o'clock if I didn't mention that. Tell Tiffany I said hey."

Zoey stared down at the phone after they hung up. She knew Tiffany was probably vibrating with the need to know who it was and what was up, but for a moment, Zoey just enjoyed the fact that she had someone she liked who liked her back. Tonight couldn't come fast enough.

Twenty-Seven

"What the fuck am I thinking?" Dani muttered to herself as she looked down at the stove. Sadly, the baked chicken looking up at her held no answers, but at least it had the kitchen smelling delicious. Inviting Zoey to dinner had been all Daniel's idea, though the fact that he said it in front of Ava's nosy ass all but guaranteed Dani wouldn't be able to talk her way out of asking. When Jordan had joined in, she knew she was a goner. Funnily enough, it wasn't until she heard Zoey's uncertainty at the validity of the offer that Dani realized she really wanted her to come too. Maybe it was a little too soon, but what was done was done.

"Smells good in here, kiddo," Daniel said as he walked in, interrupting her thoughts. Dani jerked in place before grabbing oven mitts and grabbing the dish. It was ten to seven, and Zoey would no doubt be around in the next few minutes. Dani needed everything to be as perfect as possible. If not for having already confronted her feelings, she would no doubt have been clued in by how badly she wanted this dinner to go well.

"Thanks, Pop," she said, placing the dish on the table. She looked up in time to see Jordan launch himself through the doorway.

"Auntie Ava and Ms. Zoey are coming up the driveway."

Dani frowned before remembering she had the sides to bring to the table. By the time she had everything ready and waiting to be dug into, she heard the front door open and close, followed by laughter and voices. As soon as Zoey walked into the doorway, all of Dani's misgivings flew out the window and she couldn't help but grin.

"Aw, you cooked just for me?" Grace said when she appeared behind Ava. "You shouldn't have."

"I didn't," Dani shot back, rolling her eyes. "Ava has been rubbing off on you way too much. You're becoming just as obnoxious as her."

"I'll take that as a compliment because I'm amazing," Ava said before smiling up at Grace. Dani shook her head and turned her gaze to the person she was excited to see.

Zoey looked just as good as she had that morning when Dani had spent way too much time kissing her in her doorway. Their shower had been a bit of a wash since they spent more time kissing and exploring one another than actually getting clean. Dani was now fully certain that she was all in when it came to women, and one woman in particular. Watching Zoey, head thrown back in pleasure as the sweetest sounds tumbled from her lips, was damn near life affirming.

"Zoey," Dani breathed out as she held out a hand. When Zoey took it with no hesitation, Dani couldn't help the way her grin grew. "I'm glad you could come."

"I'm glad you invited me," Zoey said, her smile just as wide, and it was like the sun was rising in their kitchen instead of setting outside their windows. Her gaze fell on the table and her eyes widened. "Wow. This looks amazing."

Dani tried not to puff her chest out and preen about her efforts being appreciated, but she could tell from Ava and Grace's snickers that she hadn't quite succeeded. Still, she didn't give a shit what they had to say about it when Zoey was gazing around like Christmas had come early.

"Thanks. Come sit and let's eat."

Dani led Zoey to the table, happy when she sat down in the chair beside her. Ava decided not to comment thankfully, and soon enough, the conversation was flowing as they all filled their plates and their mouths with food. Dani felt warmth infuse her chest as she observed Zoey, enjoying the way she put her whole body into telling stories, her hands alive in a type of interpretive dance conveying even more meaning to her words. She fit right in, surprisingly matching Ava in wit, no doubt due to the nature of both of their work. When Dani caught Grace's eye, they both exchanged semihelpless smiles. If not for that, Dani might have missed the small bit of metal on

Grace's left hand. She frowned before looking at Ava's hand and seeing a matching one.

"Oh, shit." The conversation halted at Dani's words, and everyone turned to look at her in confusion.

"What's wrong, Dani?" Zoey asked. She put a hand on Dani's arm and if not for Dani's shock, she would have melted into that warm touch.

Dani shook her head. She wasn't sure how to answer that, not when she needed to confirm something very important. She pointed at Ava. "Those two have matching rings on. Why do you have matching rings on?"

Ava blinked quickly before a sly smile spread on her face. "Well," she said drawing out the word until Dani swore she was leaning forward. Abruptly, Ava held up her hand. "Grace and I are engaged. And we're moving in together."

Dani's mouth fell open. She had expected something like this to come soon, but she hadn't been prepared for this at all. "Is this why you wanted Zoey at dinner with us?" Dani asked, trying to give herself time for the new information to pierce her brain. "To make the announcement?"

Ava and Grace glanced at one another before nodding. "Vini isn't back for another two weeks, but we couldn't wait." Ava reached out, taking Grace's ring hand in hers. "Actually, there was a double proposal. I hadn't known she was going to ask me, and I tried asking her first."

"Yeah." Grace jumped in, giving Ava a soft smile. "She

tried to stop me from asking because she wanted to ask first."

"That's because I started to speak first but we got interrupted," Ava insisted.

"Well, whoever asked first," Daniel cut in, staving off their bickering. "Congratulations. I'm so happy for the two of you."

Ava smiled. "Thanks, Pop." She turned to look up at Grace, and Dani's chest clenched. There was no denying the strength of love in Ava's gaze. If not for being so happy for them, Dani would have gouged her own eyes out. The two of them were so perfect for one another that it almost hurt to see.

"Congratulations, sis," Dani said, her voice choking up briefly. The sting in her eyes gave away just how much she felt about everything. Life had a way of showing her that changes were happening, and she was realizing how caught off guard she felt. It was good. Ava deserved to move forward after so many years of holding herself back. And maybe since she was, it was okay for Dani to as well.

Warmth touched her leg and Dani blinked quickly before looking down. When she saw a hand on her thigh, she followed it up to Zoey's concerned gaze. She was smiling but her eyes seemed to be asking if Dani was okay, and in that instance, she realized she was. Change wasn't always a bad thing. Dani covered Zoey's hand with her own and gave her a small smile and nod.

"What's going on over there?" Ava asked, breaking into the moment. Her grin was knowing as she gestured between Dani and Zoey with her fork. "What's with the looks between you two?"

Dani snorted at Ava's nosy questions, but before she could second-guess herself, she lifted her and Zoey's entwined hands. "Nothing is going on. I'm just having a quiet moment with my girlfriend, you nosy little shit."

"Mom said a bad word. That's a dollar to the swear jar," Jordan said, not looking up from his plate. Dani looked over at him and when he glanced up at her, she couldn't stop the giggle from bubbling up from her. When the laughter started, she let it tumble from her lips unimpeded, taking with it the heaviness she had been feeling and leaving only the light excitement for the future. Dani squeezed Zoey's hand and laughed harder when she felt a gentle squeeze back.

Twenty-Eight

"So, it seems like that went well," Zoey said, broaching the subject of dinner once the door to Dani's room had been closed behind them. She sat gingerly on the edge of the bed, not sure if she should make herself comfortable or if she should say good night and head home. Outside of high school, she had never slept over in someone's house when they lived with their parent or family. What were the protocols for this? She knew that multigenerational families were a thing, but it just wasn't something she had any firsthand practical experience with.

Dani's chuckle was soft but filled with humor as she leaned against the closed door. "It did seem that way, huh." She glanced away with a slight smile on her face. "It all just seems so easy with you."

Zoey wasn't sure what that was supposed to mean. "Easy how?"

Dani pushed off the door and walked toward her. Zoey tried to keep her gaze on Dani's face but the way she moved didn't have any hesitation. Her hips seemed to sway to a song that spoke directly to Zoey's soul, and she found herself listing to one side and then the next in response. When Dani was in front of her, not reaching out wasn't an option. Zoey wrapped a hand around one of Dani's wrists, gently tugging her farther forward as she parted her thighs to give her space to stand.

With her free hand, Dani reached up and brushed her fingers over Zoey's cheek, making her shiver. Zoey spared a thought to the rest of the Williams family and hoped that the walls weren't thin. She figured Dani knew better than her what could and couldn't be heard in her room, and contented herself with the thought that if she couldn't hear anyone else then they couldn't hear her either. When warmth coated Zoey's cheek, she leaned into it, luxuriating in the feeling of heat and comfort. She turned her head slightly, kissing Dani's palm. A thumb brushed over her lips and Dani opened her eyes in time to see Dani leaning in.

When their lips met, Zoey could still taste a hint of wine and the brownie they'd had for dessert. It was a decadent, lush flavor that coated her tongue and made her groan as she pulled Dani closer. When she felt a push on her shoulder, she went with it, falling back onto the bed and grunting when Dani fell against her. When Zoey opened her eyes, the sight of Dani above her illuminated by the light was enough to make her breath hitch, but she needed to know what Dani meant by her last words.

She reached a hand up and cupped Dani's cheek as she repeated her question.

"Easy how?"

Dani paused for a moment, staring down at her. Zoey thought that she might not reply until she turned into Zoey's hand, her lips brushing over her skin as she answered. "Easy like breathing." Soft kisses pressed into Zoey's palm had her stomach clenching. When Dani opened her eyes again, the heat in them had Zoey's skin damp with sweat. "Liking you. Being with you. Touching you."

Dani brushed fingers over the sensitive skin of Zoey's neck, and she leaned her head back shivering at the feeling.

"You just fit so well," Dani continued, as if her words weren't coating Zoey's soul and sending her nerves scattering like fireworks. "It makes me want to be selfish and keep you."

The gentle possessiveness of that statement lit Zoey up like a candle flame and she pulled Dani's face down to hers. "You can. Keep me, I mean. I want that."

Dani's smile was something beautiful to behold and Zoey could only take a few moments of it before she had to taste it for herself. Their kisses started slow and sweet, but when Dani's tongue brushed against Zoey's bottom lip, all bets were off. Zoey took the invitation for what it was, pressing closer and chasing that addictive taste back to its source.

Dani's weight was grounding but when Zoey felt a thigh slide between her thighs, she pulled back. The groan Dani let out was dirty, setting Zoey's blood aflame. She almost said to hell with it until she remembered where they were. "We should stop. What if someone hears us?"

Dani chased her lips. "Ava is gone back to Grace's and Pop took Jordan out for ice cream." Her hands were hot as they pressed against Zoey's skin underneath her blouse. It was an addictive feeling and almost had Zoey giving in again.

"But what if they come back before we're done?" She could hardly get her words out between the sucking kisses that were damn near devastating. She gripped Dani's hips desperately, trying to hold on to logic and sensibility when everything in her wanted to say to hell with it and get lost in the warmth and pleasure of Dani's touches. "I don't want your family to think I'm some sex-crazed degenerate."

Dani chuckled softly not letting up on her kisses. "Say that again. I love it when you use big words with me."

Zoey's words were swallowed by eager lips as her body relaxed. She wrapped her arms around Dani's waist, pulling her down fully before brushing lips to the shell of Dani's ear. "Capricious. Evocative. Mellifluous."

Dani's choked laughter was music to Zoey's ears and the full-bodied kiss she received in response to her teasing was everything she needed in life. Still, the hands that slowly stripped the clothing from her body were also appreciated and she did the same, not stopping until Dani's tacky skin was pressed against her own.

"If I had known that you were hiding all this under those cardigans, I probably would have jumped you sooner," Dani said heatedly as she pressed kisses against

Zoey's sternum. Her hands weren't idle as they lit up Zoey's nerves in their circuit from her hips to her waist.

"I wanted to kiss you against the aisles when you first asked me for book recommendations." The confession was an easy one and ended with Zoey's gasp of pleasure when she felt lips brushing over her stomach. She reached down to cup Dani's cheek, her fingers tangling with Dani's locs. Somehow, it was the feeling of them between her fingers that made this all so real.

"I probably would have let you," Dani replied, her voice muffled as she spoke against Zoey's skin. When breath brushed over the sensitive skin of Zoey's inner thigh, she had to strain to look down. The sight of Dani there so close to where she ached to be touched nearly had Zoey vibrating out of her skin. Was Dani really going to—

"What are you doing?"

The look Dani gave her was uncalled for really. "Do you really have no idea why I'm down here?"

"I know why, I'm just surprised," Zoey said, nearly breathless with need. Her chest lifted and fell in quick succession as Dani smirked before leaning closer. Zoey wanted to watch; she wanted to sear the memory in her brain. The first lick was enough to have Zoey collapsing back on the bed. "I've died and gone to heaven."

Dani's chuckle had Zoey clenching as the vibrations spread against her lips. Her legs fell open giving Dani even more room to work. Zoey reached down again, this time finding one of Dani's hands and gripping it tightly. "Let me know if I do something wrong," Dani said softly.

Zoey shook her head. "Unless you start gnawing on me, I think we'll be just fine." Her words devolved into a heated groan, and she tightened her grip on Dani's hand, intent on hanging on for the ride.

She would have thought Dani would be hesitant, but Zoey was quickly dissuaded of that notion when Dani leaned in pushing her face against the lips of her cunt. Wet slick sounds accompanied frenzied motions as Dani enthusiastically set about obliterating Zoey's ability to form a coherent sentence. It wasn't until two fingers slid in deep that Zoey came up for air and realized that for all her talk about the house potentially not being empty, she was the one making too much noise.

"Your mouth is a safety hazard," Zoey wheezed out as her thighs clenched, squeezing themselves around Dani's chest. Another devastating chuckle had her jerking in place, and she clenched her jaw to keep from crying out in pleasure. Her next moan still felt too loud even from behind clenched teeth, but there was nothing she could do about it when her mind was melting. A final glance down was enough to do it for her and Zoey nearly bit her tongue as she ran face first into her orgasm.

The wet sounds of Dani's tongue and lips against her slowly died down and she moved away when Zoey whined and tried to move. Her hands grabbed at Dani pulling her up until she could cover her lips. Their kisses were languid as Zoey sought out her own taste on Dani's tongue.

"I don't know what fantasies taught you that, but I think we need to collaborate on a book and write them down," Zoey said, breathless. Their legs tangled together as cool air brushed over their skin. Dani's smile was radiant enough to warm the room and Zoey didn't bother stopping herself from tasting it for herself.

The kitchen was bathed in warm orange as Dani flipped a pancake on the stove. Beside her, Zoey poked at the strips of bacon she was overseeing. It was still a bit surreal to her that she had spent the night in Dani's arms. They had barely finished showering when the front door opened downstairs. Zoey had hidden out in Dani's room, still a bit shy at being in a household with more than just one family member. It was a far cry from growing up with just Mason.

Dani had woken her up with soft kisses that she knew would make her spoiled. She could see herself refusing to be woken up any other way in the near future. They had spent some time trading soft kisses in the warm sunlight before Dani had groaned and pulled them both downstairs to make breakfast.

"I promised Pop I would make a whole spread, especially since Grace and Ava are coming back over."

Dani's words had been enough to get Zoey moving, as had been the little extra wiggle in her hips as she walked out of the room. Zoey was whipped and she wasn't even mad about it.

A creak on the steps had Zoey straightening. Dinner had gone well last night, but it would take some time for her to get used to this. A soft kiss on her cheek had her looking over to see Dani smiling softly at her.

"Nervous?"

She shrugged. "A little. This is the first time I've ever been invited in like this."

Dani stared at her for a moment before putting the spatula down. She stepped closer to Zoey before wrapping arms around her waist. "Well, consider this the first and last time you ever need to be invited."

"Really?"

"Yup. Once we Williams sisters find someone we like, we don't let them go that easily." Dani smiled widely. "I hope that's alright."

Zoey grinned as warmth spread through her chest. "That sounds perfect to me." She leaned in, warmth building when their lips met again in a soft kiss. It was a kiss promising a lot of things, but most importantly that they wouldn't be alone.

"Is breakfast ready yet?" Jordan's voice had them pulling apart, but neither of them moved very far. Jordan didn't look the least bit concerned, but Dani almost jumped when his eyes widened. "If you're dating Zoey, does this mean I get to check out all the books I want?"

Zoey blinked for a moment before she glanced at Dani with a smile that lit the room. "I think that can be arranged."

★ ★ ★ ★ ★

If you liked The Secret Crush Book Club,
*don't miss this other sapphic romance from
Meka James and Afterglow Books!*

Love and Sportsball

Hard work has Khadijah Upton starting her dream
job as an athletic trainer for the Atlanta Cannons.
Then an evening of celebratory letting loose turns
into a one-night stand with a beautiful stranger. It's a
reckless, wildly sexy encounter that Khadijah intends
to forget...until her first day on the job lands her
face-to-face with basketball star Shae Harris again.

Shae is a major player in every sense of the word,
and Khadijah doesn't plan to be the latest in a long
line of "Harris Honeys." Personal and professional
just don't mix. But Shae, who's all about living life
to the fullest, keeps tempting Khadijah to blur the
boundaries. And the more Shae reveals about herself,
the harder it is for Khadijah to resist her.

In the bedroom, their tension sizzles. On the
court, it's a liability. But unless Khadijah's willing
to really let Shae in, it won't be just the team cham-
pionship on the line, but a body-and-soul connection that rewrites all the rules.

Get 2 Free Books!

We'll send you 2 free books PLUS a free Mystery Gift.

Try **afterglow books**—the perfect subscription for sizzling-romance lovers! Get more great books like this delivered right to your door!

FREE Value Over $30